Two for Protection

Alaskan Tigers: Book Seven

Marissa Dobson

Published by Sunshine Press
Printed in the United States of America
ISBN-13: 978-1-939978-42-4

Dedication

To my readers who wanted to see more of the Kodiak Bears, here's your chance to explore Thaddeus' story. Also know the other Brown brothers will get their stories soon, follow my website www.marissadobson.com to stay up to date with the series so you don't miss them.

Thank you for all your support. Enjoy this newest adventure to Alaska.

Two for Protection: Alaskan Tigers

Contents

Two for Protection: Alaskan Tigers

Murder...

Courtney Mathews was in the wrong place at the wrong time when she witnessed two murders. After going to the authorities her life is turned upside down, and she's forced to flee back to her hometown in Alaska to save herself.

Mistakes...

Tad Brown is third in line to take over his sleuth—bear clan— but his mistakes cling to every decision, making him question himself. Finding Courtney forces him to confront his past in order to embrace his future. Will he be able to put the past where it belongs, and keep Courtney safe, or will it cause him to lose the woman he's destined to be with?

Changes...

With so many people depending on Milo, he must come into his own. Stepping into a role of authority has him doubting himself. Never before had he wanted to be a leader, content as one of the Elders guards. On a mission for the Alaskan Tigers, the three of them must work together to survive, with Milo taking the lead.

Two for Protection: Alaskan Tigers

Chapter One

The snow was coming down faster than the windshield wipers could keep up with it. Courtney Mathews tightened her grip on the steering wheel, afraid she wouldn't make it the last five miles to her mother's ranch. Alaskan winter driving was nastier then she remembered. Years of living in a small town in Texas had dulled her reflexes, making it harder to keep the vehicle on the road. It had been more than a dozen years since she had driven in snow, let alone blizzard conditions.

Turning around or stopping until the weather passed wasn't possible, since Nome was too far removed from civilization to have any place for her to seek shelter. She forged ahead, hoping the situation wouldn't worsen.

She was scared and alone, and her mother didn't even know she was coming. The word of her supposed death had probably reached her mother by now, leaving no one to know she was out in the blizzard alone. After Jeffery Park blew up her house, she ditched her cell phone in the burning remains, hoping everyone thought she was dead. It might keep her safe until she could make a plan and get in touch with the United States Marshal in charge of her protection. So far, witness protection wasn't turning out as she had expected.

After agreeing to testify against Jeffery Park, she was told her life wouldn't change in the least bit. On the contrary, she had to take a sabbatical from her job due to the danger that followed her everywhere. Her beautiful house was nothing but ashes, and her friends had abandoned her after the last attack on her life. Now she was running home, about to put her mother in danger because she didn't know what else to do.

Steering the car around the bend, she wasn't expecting to see a moose in the middle of the road, just lying there. She tugged the steering wheel hard to the left in an effort to avoid the large animal, and the car skidded on black ice, sending it sliding across the road, spinning around and around until she thought she'd be sick. She jolted forward when the car slammed into the ditch, and her head hit the steering wheel as pain shot up her arm.

No one will ever find me.

It had been miles since she'd seen another driver, and she would freeze to death before anyone stumbled upon her. Darkness settled around her, stealing away her thoughts and any hope she had of saving herself.

* * *

Even for Alaska, the blizzard came up quicker than Thaddeus Brown expected. Only three miles to go before he made it to the house. Thanks to his shifter eyesight, he was able to see through the heavy, wet snow coming down and his large four by four truck handled well.

When he came around the curve and saw a little red two-door car sticking out of the ditch, he balked.

"What the hell were they thinking driving *that* in this weather?"

He parked the truck and jumped out. Snow was already piling up on and around the car, making the situation dire. No one could survive these temperatures for long, even with the proper winter gear.

He slid down the embankment, keeping his feet under him and his hand on the top of the car, swiping off the snow as he went until he could see inside. Slouched over the wheel was an unconscious woman. He pulled open the door, and the wind rushed around them sending snow and ice into the vehicle.

"Ma'am?"

He reached in, placing his fingers to her throat and checked for a pulse. Electricity poured through him, telling him he'd found his mate. It seemed fainter than he expected, but pushed the thought away and focused on the exposed skin under his fingers. She was cold, but the faint pulse beating against his fingers gave him hope. Warmth was what she needed, and there wasn't a chance a medical team would come up the mountain, since his vehicle was the last they'd allowed through before they closed the roads. He had to get her to safety.

He heard a soft moan and almost thought it was the wind. Then her eyelids fluttered.

"Please…"

He saw fear in her eyes as she pulled away from his fingers, which were still pressed to her throat.

Even with the panic pouring off her, she was beautiful. Her heart shaped face, her cheeks red from the cold, stole his breath.

"Ma'am, can you hear me? I need to know if you're hurt."

"Please don't hurt me." Her eyes drifted shut again. "I don't want to die. Please, I won't testify. Just let me live."

"I'm here to help you, to get you somewhere warm." His words were wasted as unconsciousness swept over her again. The terror in her eyes warned him someone had hurt her before, making the bear within him furious.

What—or who—was she running from? He didn't have time to figure it out. He needed to get her somewhere warm. He assumed she hadn't broken any bones, since she'd been able to move away from him, so he scooped her into his arms, letting her head fall against his shoulder before he moved up the embankment to his idling truck. His footsteps from only minutes ago were nearly covered.

He loved the way she felt against his body, as if she belonged there. He had to stop his hands from wandering along her perfect curves. She was a true woman, one he didn't have to worry about breaking with his strength or weight.

He managed to get the door open without dropping her, and the heat from within rushed at him and melted the snow that had gathered on his shoulders. Placing her gently on the seat, he grabbed his jacket from where he had thrown it after the truck heated and wrapped it around her. The heavy jacket and the truck's heater would help warm her until he got her to the house.

After doing all he could for her, he dashed back to secure her car and gather whatever belongings he could find that she might need. He grabbed her keys from the ignition, looked around and found nothing but a change of clothes with the tags still on the garments, and a wallet on top. The rest of the car was spotless, clearly a rental.

He glanced at the plane ticket stub he'd found on top of the clothes; she'd flown from California, which explained why she was out in this blizzard. A local would have returned home before the roads got this bad. The new clothes told him it wasn't a planned trip. What brought her here in such a rush?

He gathered everything together, locked the car, and turned back to the road. At the top of the embankment he noticed a wolf on the hill, watching him. The wind turned, bringing the scent of a shifter toward him.

"Tate, is that you?" he called out.

Staying perched on the hill, the silver wolf tipped his head back and howled in acknowledgement.

"I'm up at Lisa's house, if you want some company or anything." Thaddeus opened the door to the truck and climbed in. Placing the woman's belongings on the middle armrest, he looked over at his unconscious passenger.

When she woke, he had some questions for her. He put the truck in gear, and continued up the road. It wasn't long before the sprawling red brick rancher came into view. It stood out against the white snow like a lighthouse beckoning to a sailor on a dark night. It was a beacon of hope and safety from the storm.

The woman beside him moaned and started to roll over until she realized she wasn't in bed.

"What the hell?" Her eyelids shot open.

"It's all right, we're almost there. Just relax, and once we're there I'll take a look at your injuries."

"Please, whatever you want, just don't kill me." She moved against the door, trying to find the handle without taking her gaze from him.

"I don't know what you're running from, but I'm not here to hurt you. If I wanted you dead, I'd have left you in the car on the side of the road to freeze to death. What the hell are you doing out in a blizzard like this anyway?" He turned onto the driveway leading up to the house, and she jolted when the truck skidded on some ice.

"Getting away. What are we doing here? How did you know?"

"Know what? This is a friend's place. She asked me to look in on it while she's away. I had a break in what I was dealing with, and planned to take a few days off here. Another friend, Milo, should be getting here at some point. Now that you know why I'm here, it's your turn."

"Where's the woman who lives here? Lisa. What have you done to her?"

He parked the truck next to the garage and turned to face her, frustration eating at him from her constant accusations. After rescuing her, he thought she'd be grateful.

"What is it about me that makes you think I'm some asshole that could hurt women?"

She avoided his question, and repeated hers again. "Where's Lisa?" She glanced around the grounds, her eyes wild with apprehension.

"Not that it's any of your business, but she's in Florida with a friend of hers." He opened the door and glanced back at her. "Shall I carry you, or can you walk?"

"I'm not going inside with you. I demand you take me…"

He cut her off with a wave of his hand. "Take you where? Have you not seen the blizzard? This isn't going to let up for a while. Now you're going inside even if I have to carry you. I will not have you freeze to death in my truck after I just hauled your ass out of a ditch. Now grab your things and get out, we're going inside." The words were harsh and true; no one would make it far in this weather. He stepped out of the truck and grabbed the two duffle bags from the backseat.

The snow crunched under his weight, his black boots leaving deep grooves in the fresh snow. He shut the door and strolled to the house, knowing she'd follow him. She was scared out of her mind, the bear inside him enjoying it, but she'd follow him in, and then he could find out what she was hiding.

Reaching down, he swept a snowdrift away from the door. He didn't turn when the truck door open behind him. Satisfied the snow wouldn't fall into the house, he rose and slipped the key into the lock and opened the door.

"How do you have a key?"

"I told you the owner is a friend of mine, and she asked me to look in on the house while she was away. Another friend of mine, Tate, lives just over the hill, and he's caring for the animals." The door opened to the mudroom where he stripped off his snow-covered boots before continuing into the house. When he flipped a light switch, nothing happened. "Shit. Electricity is down, I'll get the generator started, but the heater isn't hooked into it. Lisa normally uses the fireplaces when she's here, so she never bothered. Just hang your coat on the hook, I'll get a fire started and this place will be warm in no time."

"The electricity is always out in a storm like this. I can't believe she went to Florida and didn't bother to tell me." She kicked off her shoes and followed after him.

"You know Lisa Mathews then?" He tossed his bags on the table and quickly moved to the fireplace. Tate had helped look after the house while Thaddeus was helping the Alaskan Tigers in Texas, knowing when he'd returned the house would be ready. The cabinets and refrigerator were stocked, and wood was stacked neatly by the fireplace. It was cozy, and just what he needed after the fight in Texas.

The woman's words surprised him, but he didn't show it.

"She's my mother." She dropped her stuff on the table next to his and sat there. "I don't know you though. How long have you known her?"

He lit the kindling and began placing wood in the large river stone fireplace. "Years. Tate and his mother are friends of my family. I met Lisa through them on one of my visits. When I grabbed your belongings from the car, I found the plane ticket in the name of Tina West. I know she doesn't have a daughter by that name. Don't lie to me, who are you really?"

"It's a long story."

A knock pounded on the door and he watched her entire body tense. He turned to toss another log into the fireplace.

"It's just Hazel, Tate's mom. She must have seen my truck coming up the mountain, she's probably just stopping by to make sure I don't need anything." When he turned around, the woman was gone. He took a quick look down the hall, wondering where she went. She wasn't a shifter, but she could disappear quickly if she chose to. There was no use calling for her when he didn't even know her real name. He suspected she wasn't the Tina she pretended to be, if she was Lisa's daughter, she had to be Courtney but he wasn't sure that was true either.

He opened the front door. Hazel stood there, and Tate was in wolf form by the four-wheeler. She was a practicing witch who'd adopted Tate when he was young and orphaned. Her unique connection to shifters allowed her to help the Kodiak bears whenever they needed it, and she was also a wonderful neighbor to Lisa.

"Hazel, please come in."

"I can't stay. I just wanted to see if you needed anything. Tate mentioned you found an injured woman on the side of the road. Is she in need of healing?" Her face paled and she staggered for a moment. Tate bounded toward them with one quick jump, barking. "It's fine, I'm fine. It's just…"

"Just what, Hazel?" Thaddeus questioned, his hand on her arm to steady her.

"You've met her…your mate." Hazel ran her hand through the wolf's thick fur, then straightened. "Not until the three come together will the mating desire be released. Find your third before the man she flees from finds her if there is to be any hope of survival."

As she collapsed, her energy expended, Thaddeus caught her.

"Hazel!"

"I'm okay. I just need a minute." She took a couple deep breaths, and moved away from Thaddeus, wrapping her arm around Tate's wolf body. "You've got a lot you need to do. She's in trouble, but without the other piece to your trio, her life will be lost and possibly yours too."

"In trouble from what?" The idea of losing his mate after he had just found her made his heart stop.

"She saw something she wasn't supposed to, and he's coming after her." She brushed the snow from her body. "I should prepare, in case you need our help. Tate will keep watch, and if anyone comes around we'll be ready."

Thaddeus kept his hand on her arm, making sure she was sturdy on her feet before he let go.

"Don't put yourself in harm's way," he warned.

"We protect our own."

"Thank you."

He watched Hazel climb onto the four-wheeler and start it up. The last rays of sunlight sunk low in the horizon as the snow came down in thick clumps. Hazel had known the scared woman inside was his mate. One he was expected to share with someone unknown to either of them.

Two for Protection: Alaskan Tigers

Chapter Two

A definition of insanity…standing in the bathroom of my mother's house hiding from the neighbor. Yeah, that's at least one of them.

She leaned against the counter, cradling her injured wrist, and taking deep breaths. There had to be another option. Why hadn't she just called U.S. Marshal Quinn? Instead she'd run off by herself, bringing danger to anyone she met.

"Tina?" A deep voice traveled down the hall to her.

"Tina?" She whispered the name as her eyebrow rose at her reflection. Ribbons of blood dried down her face from the large gash by her hairline, and a bruise was starting to form around her eye. She was a mess. Opening the door, she peeked out, checking to see if there was anyone else. She'd already dragged him into her mess; she couldn't bring the neighbors into it too.

"There you are. Come sit by the fire and let me look at your arm."

Unwilling to hide in the bathroom all night, and eager for the warmth of the fireplace to chase the chill from her body, she stepped out of the bathroom. The familiar smell of home greeted her. A mixture of her mother's perfume and fresh baked cookies lingered in the air, wrapping around her like a blanket. Pictures of her childhood lined the hall, beginning with baby pictures and ending with her most recent two, graduating from college and accepting her position in Texas. All of it gave the illusion of a happy family. In reality, she'd never gotten along with her mother, hence the reason she'd taken the job in Texas leaving behind the wonders of Alaska. Despite the past, relief to be home filled her and for a brief moment replaced her fear.

"My name's not Tina." His jet-black hair and bright green eyes were the first thing she'd noticed when they were in the truck, but now she saw the deep contours of muscles under his shirt. The stubble teasing along the line of his jaw gave him a rough, manly look.

"I've gathered as much, but you haven't told me who you are yet." He went to the table where he'd tossed his bags earlier.

As she watched him, she caught a glimpse of a gun, the holster peeking out from beneath his shirt. Fear tore through her, forcing her backward. She stumbled as she tried to get away, then bumped into the wall causing a picture frame to crash the floor, sending broken glass across the rug.

"What the hell?" He spun toward her.

"You work for him…" She managed to get away from the wall, taking another step back only to have a large wedge of glass slice through her foot. Warm blood pooled in her sock and she gasped in pain.

"I work for no one. Now do you want to tell me what the hell is going on, or are you planning to stumble around in that glass until you've bled yourself dry?" He reached back and snatched the first aid kit from the bag. "My name is Thaddeus Brown, my friends call me Tad. Now come sit down and let me look at your injuries."

Tad Brown...Brown, where have I heard that name?

She wracked her memory trying to come up with the answer. It wasn't until the firelight reflected off the symbol on the first aid kit that she realized who he was. The outline of a bear head with a paw print circling it, the initials K.B. just below the bear's head. She recalled the rumors of the Brown family, assassins who could shapeshift into bears. Had Jeffery hired him to kill her?

"You're from the island..."

He nodded. "My family owns the island. Lisa told you about us?"

"No, but I know about your family. I'm Lisa's daughter Courtney, and you have no right to be here. Leave, now." She stiffened her back, trying to establish some control.

"I save you from the blizzard, and you're going to throw me into it. Ironic. You don't get your hospitality from your mother, that's for sure." He took a seat in front of the fire, the first aid kit in his lap.

"I know all about your family, and I want *nothing* to do with any of you." Throwing him out in the blizzard wouldn't kill him if what she'd heard was true.

"Ahhh, gossip at it's best, I'm sure. Not everything you hear about my family is true. Ask me whatever you want and I'll tell you what I can to put your mind at rest." He patted the seat next to him. "Let me help you."

"You're assassins. I can't trust you. Jeffery hired you to kill me, didn't he?"

"Assassin. Where would you get that idea?" He laughed, shaking his head. "I don't know anyone named Jeffery. Now sit."

"I was a reporter with Nome Report before I moved to Texas. I heard about your family while I was there. You must have someone keeping your secrets because all the stories any of the journalists turned in were squashed before they could ever be printed." She leaned against the wall, taking the weight off her injured foot.

"Can you keep a secret?" There was a spark of lightness in his eyes. "I *am* a bear shifter, that much is true. Yes, we have an insider at the Report to keep our secret from becoming public knowledge. But we are *not* assassins."

There was a truth to his words that she could feel in her bones. If he wanted to kill her, he'd had plenty of chances.

"If you're not assassins, why is it so important for you to keep your secret?"

"What do you think would happen if the public knew what my family is?" When she didn't answer, he continued. "They'd hunt us down like deer. But instead of killing us, they would capture us, put us in cages, and study us. I won't have my parents, siblings, or anyone else become lab rats. I will do what must be done to keep our secret."

"Even murder."

"I've never murdered an innocent. Nor have I been hired to murder anyone." He opened the first aid kit and looked at her again.

"You're only doing more damage to yourself. Let me attend to your wounds."

She widened her eyes with the realization he hadn't said he'd never murdered anyone, only that he never murdered an innocent. What was this man hiding? She limped across the floor just as a growl shook the house.

"What was that?"

"Milo is announcing his arrival." He sat the first aid kit aside and stood. "Sit down, I'll attend to your wounds once I've let him in."

"Who's Milo?" she called after him.

"The friend I mentioned would meet me here." He shot her a quick smile and opened the door, letting a seven-foot Bengal tiger stroll in. Snow fell from the fur as it made its grand entrance.

"You've got to be shitting me! This can't be happening." Her legs gave out, forcing her to the nearest armchair. She dragged her hand through her auburn hair, pulling it away from her face, never taking her gaze from the tiger. She should have been scared, but instead all she could do was sit there with her mouth hanging open in amazement.

"Go, I'll grab your bag." It was clear he wasn't talking to her. He walked to the table, grabbing one of the bags before looking back at her. "I've got to take this to Milo so he can change. Just wait here for a moment. Then we can discuss what's happening." Tad and Milo disappeared down the hall leaving her alone.

Wow! She tugged off her sock, careful not to push the glass deeper into her foot. Digging through the first aid kit, she found the tweezers, and began to pull the shards out one by one. Every part of her hurt, her head being the worst. Damn the blizzard. She needed to get away before Jeffery found her. These people didn't deserve to be dragged into her mess, and neither did her mother. Where was she going to go? This was the last place she thought Jeffery would look for her.

Not to mention the fact she was stuck in a house with two shifters. People she never thought existed. Legends, rumors, books, and even movies all claimed they did, but she'd never bought into it. Now that she'd seen Milo in his tiger form, she couldn't deny it any longer. The danger following her might be nothing compared to what followed them. As Tad told her, anyone who knew of his kind would want them for experiments.

"Your fear is pouring from you, making you forget your pain, but the blood loss will begin to take its toll."

She looked to see Tad standing next to the chair. "It's fine. I've got the glass out and the bleeding has stopped. I just need to bandage it."

"Your head wound." He tipped his head to her. "They bleed a lot Let me clean it and close it."

Pain seared through her when she touched the spot. When she brought her hand away, her fingers were coated in blood. "Okay." She nodded, giving him permission to come closer.

He grabbed some gauze. "Hold this to your forehead." She did as he asked and he readied the cleaning supplies. "Can you move your wrist?"

"It's not broken, just badly sprained." She met his gaze. "It's not safe for me to be here, I need to go."

"I'm pretty sure we already established that no one is going anywhere. The blizzard is going to last for the next few days. Planes are grounded, roads are closed, we are on our own here. Nome is cut off from the rest of the world until this passes."

Another man walked into the room. "If you're in trouble you're going to have to trust us. I'm Milo. How about you tell me who you are."

She looked up at him. Milo seemed intimidating at first, but the white dress shirt and jeans made him more approachable. His dark hair was nearly the same shade as Tad's, but his eyes were different. Milo's were a crystal blue, full of light, love, and warmth. It wasn't until he stepped completely out of the shadows that she saw the shoulder holster and gun, pushing the fear back to the forefront of her mind again.

"I'm Courtney, Lisa's daughter." She cringed as Tad cleaned her wound, pain sending black spots through her vision. She tried to focus on Tad to force the spots away. "You told me you weren't a murderer, so why do you both have guns?"

"Protection, nothing more. I told you what people would do to catch us. It's a dangerous time for our kind right now." He used a butterfly bandage to keep the wound together. "Courtney, you're going to need to trust us."

"We can feel your fear as if it was our own," Milo explained as he came closer. "It teases along the air until it feels like it'll choke me. What are you running from?"

"Something bad, real bad." She shook her head and tried not to think about everything she'd lost so far. "Being around me is dangerous for you. If you live close or can go to your friend's house, you should before *they* find me."

Tad and Milo shared a look before shaking their heads. Tad laid his hand over hers. "Not happening. That's no way to repay Lisa. Now *they*, as in this Jeffery you mentioned before and who else?"

"Jeffery Park, he'll see me dead before I can testify against him." Her body shook with memories of the night that got her into this situation. "He's why I ran, why I came home. I didn't want to put Mom in danger but I didn't know where else to go. When they blew up my house, I hoped I would be pronounced dead and he wouldn't keep hunting me."

"Tell us why he's after you." Milo came and knelt next to her. "We can keep you safe, but we need to know what we're up against."

"No one can protect me. The U.S Marshal that was assigned to me was killed. I was waiting for the reassigned one, Quinn. He was on his way when…" She took a deep breath. "Jeffery is the U.S. contact for a drug smuggling operation. He accepts the deliveries and distributes them. I was covering the story about the increase in drugs on the streets, when I saw him murder two of the dealers for not making their minimal sells. I went to the police. I knew I would be in danger, but I thought they would keep me safe. Keep him locked up until the trial…but he's out on bail. I can't believe a man like that can be out, with all the evidence against him. What is our legal system coming to if he can kill two people and be out on bail? It's not just my word, there's DNA evidence." She knew she was rambling, but it felt good to finally be able to tell someone.

"It's okay, we'll keep you safe." Tad ran his fingers over her knuckles. "The system doesn't always work like we want or need it to. If he has connections or enough money then bail can be given. It doesn't matter, nothing is going to happen to you."

"You can't protect me against him. No one can. He'll kill from a distance. By the time you know he's there, it'll be too late."

Tad shook his head. "No, it won't. We'll be able to smell him before he gets near you. You just need to relax."

"It wouldn't be U.S. Marshal Quinn Evans, would it?" Milo inquired.

"Yes. Do you know him?"

Milo nodded. "I'll contact him to let him know you're safe and see where things stand." He laid his hand on her leg and the connection flared to life.

A tingling warm sensation shot through her, opening her up completely to the both of them. It was like a current of electricity was moving through her, connecting the three of them together. She looked at them expecting them to be glowing from all the power that tingled through them.

"What's happening?" she asked, her voice timid.

Two for Protection: Alaskan Tigers

Chapter Three

Milo's eyes widened with the knowledge of what was happening, and he glanced at Tad to confirm it. The emotions of Tad and Courtney flowed through him, making his stomach roil with the sudden rush, and the chocking terror Courtney was dealing with. Unable to pull his hand away, he sank to the floor trying to believe it.

Mates. A human and bear.

"Tad?"

Tad's deep inhale cut through the air like a knife. "Do you believe in soul mates? Love at first sight?"

Her green eyes sparkled with unshed tears. "I guess. I've never really thought about it. My mom said when she met my father there was an instant connection. What does this have to do with anything? What just happened?"

Milo squeezed her thigh, bringing her attention back to him. "It's hard to explain, Courtney, and it sounds unbelievable. Shifters have something like what humans consider soul mates. When we find ours, a connection is formed, linking us together. It's what has happened here."

"That's insane."

He tucked a strand of hair behind her ear. "Insane as it must sound to you, it's true. It's our life."

"You can feel our emotions as I felt your fear earlier." Tad leaned forward, closer to her. "If you don't believe what Milo says, believe what you feel. You feel drawn to us, do you not?"

She shook her head, bumping into Milo's hand. "I felt the draw to you before, but that means nothing. I wanted comfort, someone to help me. There's nothing supernatural about desire between two...well, three consenting adults."

Tad and Milo exchanged another glance. "Desire, no...but the mating is," Tad explained. "It's also something you won't be able to fight. The longer you go without the touch of your mates, the more painful it becomes. There are key differences in the human idea of love at first sight and shifters mating."

She cocked her head to the side and raised an eyebrow at him. "What are you saying?"

"That you won't be able to resist us." Milo's fingers teased along her jaw. "Every second that passes ties us closer together. Denying a mate's touch is more than longing. It will send agony through your body until it breaks your mind."

Easing out of their touch, she stood and strolled to the window, a slight limp from the cuts on her foot slowing her. "This isn't happening, I'm running for my life and now two shifters show up and try to lay their claim to me."

"I understand this is hard to believe, but the timing couldn't be better." When she spun around to glare at Milo, he explained. "Being mates we will always know if you're in danger, wherever you are. We will protect you from Jeffery and anyone he hires. No harm will come to you as long as we're here."

"You can't promise that. The U.S. Marshal was supposed to do that, instead he ended up dead. I don't want to see others killed because of me." Tears glistened in her eyes as she met Milo's gaze.

He stood from where he knelt by the chair, careful to not scare her he closed the distance between them. "Nothing will happen to us. Shifters are harder to kill." Tentatively, he touched her, drawing his finger down her arm.

"You don't understand what kind of man Jeffery is. He'll kill anyone who gets in his way. No one around me is safe. He blew up my house trying to stop me."

Tad came to them, standing on her other side. He slid his arm around her waist, linking them together again through touch. "Trust me, we've gone up against worse than him. If he blew up your house and killed the U.S. Marshal in charge of keeping you safe, how did you escape?"

"I was in the garage getting a jar of pasta sauce from the storage area…since the pantry is too small. So I made a secondary one just off the garage door." She realized she was getting away from the point and shook her head. "The Marshal was in the kitchen on the phone, making arrangements for Quinn to take over so he could attend a court date when it happened. I was thrown across the room and landed next to the outside door. I ran outside with the hopes of saving him but the house was completely engulfed in flames. There was no way in. I did the only thing I could think of and ran."

"Do you believe anyone saw you?" Tad asked.

"I don't think so, but...I don't know, I just ran. I didn't know where else to go, so I headed for Mom's. Tina is a friend of mine, that's why I used her name. We could be twins, so she gave me her ID and passport so I could get here."

Milo put his forefinger under her chin, gently gliding it up until she looked at him. "You did the right thing. Everything is going to be fine." Unshed tears still glistened in her eyes. His words didn't convince her, only time would. "I'll call Quinn and let him know you're safe. He won't be able to get here until after the blizzard lets up, but unless Jeffery followed you when you left he won't be here until then either. You're safe for now."

* * *

For now. Those two little words sent a cold chill through her. Tad stood by the window, his arm still around her waist, and she felt herself relax into him. It was insane, but his touch seemed to chase away some of her fears and provided the comfort she so desperately wanted.

Both of the men were intimidating, their large bulky frames full of toned muscles that scared her and provided comfort at the same time. Just looking at them should have sent her running in the opposite direction. Instead, each touch was soft and comforting, something she wouldn't have expected.

"Will you let me wrap your wrist now to keep the swelling down?" Tad asked.

With the mention of her wrist, it began to throb again. The swelling was nearly as bad as the deep purple and yellow bruise forming. To once again make sure nothing was broken she rotated her wrist, sending pain shooting up her arm.

"Okay."

"It's a bad sprain and will take time to heal, but considering everything you've been through it's minor compared to what it could have been." He guided her back to the first aid kit in front of the roaring fire, and they sat on the soft velvety sofa.

"Double injury to it made things worse." He gazed at her and the question was clear in his eyes.

"I hurt it in the blast when he bombed my house. It wasn't too bad, but I must have made it worse with the car accident."

"You shouldn't have been out in weather like this, not with that little car." Tad grabbed one of the wraps from the kit and sat down next to her.

"That's all the rental place had and I had to get to Mom's." She laughed; the whole situation seemed ridiculous now. "Turns out Mom wasn't even here. If you hadn't come along I wouldn't have been able to get in. My keys are somewhere in the crispy remains of my house in Texas. My house…" The tears she had put off for so long rolled down her face.

"It's all right, houses can be rebuilt. The important thing is that you're okay." He wrapped her wrist with care.

"I lost everything. My beautiful house, my job…"

"You found us." He clasped the wrap shut and gently took both of her hands in his.

She wasn't sure what she would have said to Tad's comment. Thankfully, Milo chose that moment to come back into the room and she didn't have to worry about it.

Milo placed his cell phone on the coffee table before sitting down next to her. "Quinn is glad you're in safe hands, and wants us to stay put until he can get here."

Being between them again made her feel warm and safe. A feeling she hoped would last, at least until this whole threat was over. Once Quinn arrived, he'd probably rush her off to some safe house where she'd go stir crazy until the trial.

"Then what?"

"That's what I wanted to talk to you both about." Milo placed his hand on her leg. "Quinn knows what Tad and I are because he's a shifter as well. He has to keep his second nature to himself or not only risk losing his job but also exposing our kind. It made it easier for me to explain things to him. I want to take you home to Fairbanks."

"Home? With you?"

"With us. Tad has been helping my clan with…security. It's the safest place for you, safer than any safe house they can put you in. It will be impossible for Jeffery to get to you once you're at the compound."

Tad gave a brief but deep laugh. "I think we should explain. She already thinks my family is a bunch of assassins, so that little comment about security only makes her question it more."

"I…I don't. Well, not any longer," she insisted.

"That's generous, but I'm sure you still have lingering doubts." Tad drew his thumb over her knuckles. "Years ago when the Alaskan Tigers, Milo's clan, came here, my family was having some issues with some rogue shifters. Ty, the Alaskan Tigers' Alpha, helped clear things up, and since then my family and the Tigers have joined together for the common good. Even more so now that Tabitha, the Queen of the Tigers and Ty's mate, has rejoined the clan. We have fought side by side to eliminate the threats to our kind and to humans."

"That all sounds past tense," Courtney noted.

"We just took down the former Alpha of the Texas Tigers, and have replaced the leader of the Texas clan with one of our own. However, with Tabitha declaring herself as the Queen of the Tigers, it is likely that things will begin to stir up more before they calm down. I've been spending more time at the compound than on my family's island at the request of my brothers."

"Brothers?"

"Taber and Thorben. They're the oldest, and they've mated with one of the clan's females, Kallie," Tad explained. "They have made their home at the compound. Bears are bigger than tigers, we're more impressive in our animal forms, and we use that to our benefits."

Maybe not assassins, but still on the wrong side of the law. She had a brief moment to wonder what she'd gotten herself into before Tad spoke again.

He raised an eyebrow at her, but the corners of his lips were curved into a half smile. "I felt that thought."

She swallowed, and tried not to show her worry. "You're a mind reader now?"

"No, not a mind reader, but mates can feel what you feel. It gave me a hint as to what you were just thinking."

"He's right. Even I caught that, and it wasn't directed at me." Milo spoke for the first time since Tad started his story.

"Then what was I thinking?" Her stomach turned with apprehension. If he knew what she was thinking and feeling, how was she going to be able to keep anything a secret?

"That I was still on the wrong side of the law for your tastes," Tad said. "That's not completely true, after all there's no law about shifters. We don't kill humans. I've only killed shifters who are rogue. Rogues kill *both* of our kinds. To leave them alive is a threat to all of us."

Milo cleared his throat. "We're getting off topic here. Neither Tad, nor myself, or either of our clans are assassins. You could call us protectors if you like. I'd like you to come back to the compound because it's the safest place for you, and because we will both have to return there."

"If the compound is just outside of Fairbanks, why are you here?"

"Years ago I was hunting a rogue with my Lieutenant, when I was attacked from behind." Milo's eyes were downcast. "He sliced through nerve endings in my shoulder, and because I wasn't able to shift right away they never healed properly. The fighting in Texas caused it to flare up. My Alpha ordered me to take a few days off to give my shoulder a break before I did more damage to it." He looked back up at Courtney. "Tad mentioned he needed to check on the house and asked me if I wanted to tag along for a few days. Within the clan, I'm a guard for the Lieutenant's mate, Bethany, and my days off are few and far between, so this sounded heavenly." He rotated his shoulder, as if just mentioning it had sent a twinge of pain through him.

Two for Protection: Alaskan Tigers

Chapter Four

After dinner, Courtney was still uneasy, the hairs on the back of her neck standing straight. Something was coming. Not *something*, Jeffery or one of his goons. Somewhere out in the dark, they were coming for her. Would they make it before the blizzard passed over the small sleepy town or was he already on her trail, about to corner her?

Without more evidence that Jeffery had orchestrated the attack on her home, he was still free on bail until the trial. Would she survive the next two months before the trial, or longer if his lawyers were able to get another continuance?

Tad came up next to her, placing his hand on her shoulder, massaging it gently. "You shouldn't be sitting by the window. Why don't you come over here with us?"

With us... Those two little words made her heart skip a beat.

Maybe it was a little strange being drawn to both of them, but after everything she had been through she was used to unusual occurrences. Maybe some amazing sex with these two was just what she needed to take her mind off the threat chasing her.

Down, girl. She scolded herself. She couldn't believe she had just met them and she was already thinking about getting them naked and having a one-night stand. She had never been prude, but such a thing was out of the question.

"I should try to call my mother. I don't want her to hear that I'm dead without knowing the truth."

Tad unclipped his cell phone from his jeans and handed it to her. "Her number is in the contacts, and you won't have to worry about the phone being traced. Milo and I will make some hot chocolate, and give you privacy."

"Thank you." She took the phone, and watched how the jeans moved over his butt as he walked away. The need to touch him, to run her hands over him, moving up his chest to feel the well-defined muscles under her fingers before sliding down his biceps, almost forced her from the window seat. What was happening to her? She'd never felt this level of desire for any man before, let along one she'd just met.

She forced herself to look down at the cell phone, scrolling through the contacts until she found her mother's name and pressed the call button. How was she going to explain the events that brought her to this position? Not wanting her mother to worry about her, or show up in Texas, she never said a word about what had happened, especially about Jeffery or the trial.

"How's my house, Taddybear?" Her mother's voice along with loud music came bursting through the speaker.

"Mom, it's Courtney. Who's Taddybear?" She couldn't have been talking about that little brown stuffed bear she'd had as a kid.

"Tad, of course." Her laughter died away. "What are you doing with Tad anyway? Are you at the house?"

She tried to picture how Tad reacted to being called Taddybear. "Yeah, I'm at your house. I needed a place to stay. Mom, could you step out of wherever you are? I really need to talk to you."

"Okay, one minute." She heard her mom say something to whomever she was with before the music faded. "Courtney, is everything okay?"

"No...oh, Mom. I'm just going to come out with it. You might want to sit down. A few months ago I witnessed a very powerful man murder two people..."

"What? Oh my God, did you go to the police? Why are you just telling me this?"

"You taught me well. Yes, I went to the police. The thing is, he has powerful connections, and even with my eyewitness testimony and the DNA evidence, he was able to get out on bail. Mom...he blew up my house, killing the U.S. Marshal who was there for my protection. I had nowhere else to go, so I came home."

"Oh God, are you okay? Were you hurt? I'll get a flight out right away. Until I get there, stay with Tad, he'll protect you." Her mother's words ran together, not giving Courtney a second to answer.

"No, Mom. I'm fine, please stay there where you're safe. This man might come after me, so I don't want you anywhere near me." She looked to the kitchen, catching a quick glance of the men busying themselves. "Tad and his friend Milo are here, they'll stand in as my protectors until the blizzard passes and the new U.S. Marshal Quinn arrives. I wanted to tell you because they might think I was killed in the blast, and I wanted you to know the truth in case the police contact you."

"Don't be ridiculous, girl, I'm coming home. I'll be on the first flight as soon as they open the airport into Nome, but in the meantime I'll start working my way west. I love you, sweetie. Please be safe." There was a sharp intake of breath, as though her mother was suppressing a sob. "Could you put Taddybear on?"

Courtney stood from the window seat. "Mom."

"Don't *Mom* me, young lady. I want to talk to Tad *now.*"

Her mother still made her feel like she was eight years old, not twenty-eight. "One moment." When she entered the kitchen, the men stopped whispering and turned to look at her. "She wants to speak with you." She held out the phone to Tad, wondering what she had just interrupted.

"Perfect timing, why don't you join me by the fire?" Milo held two of mugs, an easy smile on his face.

She nodded and followed him, making sure she was behind him to see how he compared to Tad. Milo's jeans were low on his hips, right on the widest part of his hipbones. They were tight and hugged his ass just like Tad's did, but the sway was more irresistible if that was possible. She reached out her fingers, nearly brushing against him before she caught herself. What was happening to her? She barely knew either of these men and she was letting her unbelievable desire for them take over. She was stronger than a little lust; there was no way she was going to let it control her.

"Are you going to tell me what you were talking about?"

"What if I said no?" He sat on the sofa and nodded to her to come join him.

"No?" She took the mug from him and sat down. The scent of real hot chocolate drifted to her, along with the memories of the last time she'd had the real stuff. Strangely enough, it was the last time she was home visiting her mother.

"It will only worry you more."

"Like that's possible." She rolled her eyes and let out a sigh.

"We were going over the possibilities that you were followed." He wrapped his arm her shoulders. "Told you it would make you worry more. I promise we will keep you safe."

"He's killed three people that I know of, do you really think he'll stop when he's gotten away with it so far?"

"We're going to see that he stops and that you're safe. Now let us do the worrying." He took a drink of his hot chocolate before nodding to the television. "There's no cable, but Lisa has plenty of DVDs, or we can use Tad's laptop and see if we can pick up the Internet through the storm and find something online to watch if you want."

"I don't really care. It's been so long since I've even turned my own television on." Mentioning her mom made her glance toward the kitchen.

"He's reassuring Lisa that you're safe."

"You can hear him?" Her gaze shifted away from Tad to Milo.

"Shifters have exceptional hearing, among other things. Your mom is worried about you and Tad's trying to calm her, not to mention trying to get her to stay in Florida at least until the blizzard passes. She is a stubborn woman."

"Tell me about it. All through my teenage years we bumped heads. It caused a gap as large as Texas between us. Now we barely talk. I didn't even know she was away. Oh God, if Jeffery goes after her…" The thought of her mom being in jeopardy because she did the right thing terrified Courtney.

"We already have that covered. Tad is going to place a call to the Alpha of the West Virginia Tiger clan, Jinx. We'll have someone accompany Lisa here, or to our compound if you agree to go with us. She'll be safe."

"How does Jinx and his clan play into your clan?" She set the mug aside and turned slightly to look at him, pulling her leg up under her.

"There are a number of clans who have partnered with my clan to form a stronger group against any resistance. The West Virginia clan was the first one, and Jinx has been with the clan almost since Tabitha joined us. He's been spending a lot of his time in Alaska helping to keep Tabitha and the compound safe. Now that he has mated, he still divides his time between Alaska and West Virginia but has for the first time appointed a Lieutenant for his clan to keep control while he's in Alaska."

"What do you mean for the first time? You mentioned your clan has a Lieutenant, so why wouldn't his have already have one?"

"Smaller clans normally only have the Alpha. The West Virginia clan is small, so there was no need for two in the position of power. Jinx isn't willing to give up his control of the clan. He's a strong man and wouldn't do well being under anyone. Plus, the clan is mostly made up of family, and it is his responsibility to be the Alpha. Once he found his mate, he promoted his brother, Lukas, to the position of Lieutenant." He teased his fingers up her leg.

"Your world is so different from mine." She wasn't sure how she would ever fit into it.

"Not that different. We have strong structure, rules, and punishments, but other than that we aren't very different. My clan is like a family, we all look out for one another. If you give it a chance and come with us, I'm sure you won't regret it. Lisa has been there, mostly before we gained healers within the clan. Her medical training helped when there was a bystander injured. Her and Doc work well together."

"How did she get drawn into the shifter world?"

"Lisa was having problems with wolves and put up traps around her land. She heard the howls of what she thought was a wolf, instead it was the neighbor Tate. He's a wolf shifter. When she went to the trap she found him freeing himself, naked in human form. He explained what he was and that's when Devon, Tad's father, was visiting. He brought your mother into our confidence, hearts, and home."

The fire cracked, sending sparks up the chimney. Her mom was always willing to help someone in needed. She was the kindest woman Courtney knew, a woman who would go out of her way for a complete stranger or an animal, let alone someone she knew and cared for. It was part of the driving wedge between them. How could her mother be there for everyone else, but when she needed something her mom was always too busy to be bothered? The thought of her mother manning the small farm by herself made her feel selfish. Did she do the right thing when she accepted the job in Texas? It was everything she'd worked for, but at what expense? The choices she'd made to get the job ended up leading her to losing her home and career all because of her values. Would she lose something more precious before it was over?

Sometime while she was deep in thought, Tad returned, and she didn't notice him until he sat down on the other side of her, his hand rubbing over the small of her back.

"I spoke with Ty. He'll have Taber standing by with the airplane for when the storm lets up. He also has a team going to Lisa's location to keep her safe."

She twisted just enough that she could look back at Tad. "I'm sorry for my mother. She shouldn't have forced you to protect me."

"She did nothing of the kind. I protect you because you're my mate. She's only worried about you and wanted to make sure you were safe. How about we take your mind off all of this?"

"What do you have in mind, Taddybear?" She couldn't help but use the nickname her mom called him.

"I guess I shouldn't be surprised Lisa mentioned the nickname." Tad rolled his eyes, and Milo chuckled. "Did she tell you why she calls me that? She only told me that in bear form I remind her of something. She says someday I'll find out the whole story."

"Oh, I know why." She grinned and leaned back, resting her back against Tad, Milo's hand still in hers. "When I was young, I had this small teddy that I carried everywhere. I'm sure it's still on my bed in my childhood bedroom. It was so tattered, but I loved it. Poor thing lost an ear from me dragging it everywhere I went. It was my Taddybear."

Tad's chest vibrated with laughter under her. "I think it's safe to assume Hazel knew and told Lisa of our destiny. She must have had a vision from touching something of yours and knew we would end up together."

"Hazel?"

"She's the neighbor, Tate's adoptive mother, and she's a witch. She has ways of knowing things, and when she stopped by earlier, she mentioned when the three of us were together that the mating desire would be released. She didn't mention Milo by name, only that he'd unleash the last dam holding back the desire." Tad laid his hand over Milo's and hers. "We're destined to be together, the three of us."

"It's hard to believe, but I can't deny the reactions from my body. It's like I have no control. I barely know either of you, but I want you both naked." She blushed. "My mind runs with fantasies."

She placed her other hand over Tad's so that both of their hands were between hers.

"Sugar, we can make all your fantasies and more come true." Milo winked at her, sending her heart fluttering.

"I have no doubt about it." She let her head fall back against Tad's shoulder. Exhaustion pulled on her, but she didn't want the night to end. She wanted to stay with them in front of the fire, watching the snow fall outside—a romantic evening. Being snowbound with two handsome men, both wanting her as much as she wanted them. If only there wasn't a threat hovering over her head, she might have taken them both to bed right then.

"Let's create a bed here in front of the fire and we can get to know each other better until you're tired," Milo suggested.

There was nothing she wanted more.

Chapter Five

Milo awoke to the sun streaming through the windows, his arm wrapped around Courtney, the back of his hand brushing against Tad's hip. It was so peaceful; there was no better way to start a day than cuddled next to one's mates. He laid there for a moment, enjoying the warmth of her body. The sweet strawberry shampoo and the faint chocolate scent from the hot chocolate still clung to her. He was tempted to snuggle back against her and sleep longer. The vibrating cell phone still clipped to his jeans announced other plans.

Slipping from the makeshift bed, he tugged the phone off his pants and brought it to his ear, walking across the room so as not disturb them.

"Milo."

"It's Quinn. There's been a development in Courtney's case. Jeffery Parks has skipped town. The judge had him surrender his passport, but he's gone. There's been a sighting of him boarding a private place yesterday, but no record of him being on the flight. The flight plan says the pilot was supposed to go to Seattle and back, but the plane never returned."

"Shit!" He glanced back at Courtney. Tad's eyes were open and he was no doubt listening to everything Quinn said.

"I've got a friend with a private plane, and he agreed to bring me. We'll get as close as we can until the storm passes. Let me know if you suspect he's there. I'd prefer not to inform the Chief of Police. Last thing we need is him finding out." It was clear Quinn was implying he didn't want the police to suspect they were shifters. "My friend is one of us, so there's nothing to worry about. He'll help if we need it."

"Okay, if you can't get here, Taber is standing by with the plane. First break in the weather, he'll be here to get us to the compound. If you don't make it before that, meet us there." Milo watched as Tad rose, moving to the window. He glanced outside, then closed the curtains.

"Keep her safe. We need her to wrap Jeffery Park up in a nice tight bow," Quinn said.

The thought of someone coming after his mate had the beast within him bubbling to the surface, ready to take off the head of anyone who dared come near her. "No worries there, no one will get near her." He growled.

"You haven't..." Quinn's tone was accusing.

"She's ours. No one will lay a finger on her. Tad and I will make sure of it. Anyone who tries to hurt our mate will be eliminated."

"Don't. I want to see him rot behind bars."

"Then you'd better get here before he comes after my mate." Milo pulled the phone away from his ear, sliding his finger across the end button, and met Tad's gaze. "You heard?"

"Yes. I'm going to check the perimeter, and then shower. Stay with her."

"Good. I'm going to update Ty with the news from Quinn." Milo sank down on the sofa, watching over Courtney while she slept. He tried to remain calm and focused while his tiger clawed at his insides. He was angry his mate was in danger while he sat there unable to do anything except wait for the attack. He wasn't someone who liked to be on the defensive; he preferred to make the moves before danger landed on his doorstep.

He pulled Ty's number up and placed the call before his beast demanded he wrap his arms around her and hold her tight until the danger found them. The phone rang and rang with no answer. He hung up, knowing Ty would call him back whenever he was free from whatever business detained him.

Courtney lay there, still deeply asleep and completely unaware of what might at this very moment be outside preparing for an attack. If Jeffery left shortly after she had, he could have made it before the blizzard was at its worst.

For the second time that morning, his cell phone pulled him away from his thoughts of her. Figuring it was Ty, he didn't bother to glance at the caller ID. Instead, he slid his finger over the screen and brought it to his ear.

"Milo."

"Ty is dealing with a shifter in Pennsylvania who wants to join a clan, possibly Korbin's in Ohio, and he asked me to call you. What's going on?" Raja's rich voice came through the phone. Even with the miles that separated them, the stress was clear in his voice. They had been dealing with a lot since Tabitha announced herself as Queen to the Tigers.

"Quinn believes Jeffery might already be here. All they know for sure is he left Texas. Supposedly he was seen boarding a plane, but there's no record of him doing so. Can you get someone in Texas to see if they can come up with any leads? Quinn is on his way, but with the airport closed he won't be able to get here quickly enough, so if he can't make it before Taber does, I asked him to meet us at the compound."

"I'll have Tex look into Jeffery. Do you want me to ask Devon or one of the other Brown brothers to come assist you and Tad? They are closer than any of us are and might be able to make it off the island."

Milo dragged his hand through his hair and considered it for a moment before shaking his head. "Not yet. If we need it, Tad can call his brothers in."

"Very well. I'll let you know if we find out anything." Raja sighed. "Not that you need the additional stress, but we've received confirmation that the Arizona Tigers have dispensed. Those loyal to our kind were killed and the rest are rogues, joining Randolph's ranks. Minnesota's Alpha is giving us some problems as well. Ty and I are working to gather the Alphas of the clans loyal to Tabitha and our kind to put a plan of action together. This is getting bigger than we expected."

"Tad has his laptop here, so let me know if there's anything I can do to help. I also might be able to help with Minnesota if it comes down to it." Randolph had taken over when Pierce was killed, heading up the rogues. Their determination to kill Tabitha was stronger than ever.

"There's nothing for you to do right now. We just need you both back and ready to work when this blizzard passes. Is Courtney going to be ready for that? Have you told her what you are?"

"Yeah, it would have been hard to keep it from her since she's Tad's and my mate. Not to mention I strolled into the house in tiger form when she first saw me. We'll make sure she's ready when the time comes. She's scared and grew up believing the rumors of Tad's family. A family of assassins, can you believe it?" Milo chuckled at the thought. All of the Brown males were intimating; they could be cold when the situation called for it, but every single one of them had a heart of gold when it came to innocents.

"I've heard those rumors. I think Devon's father started it to keep intruders off the island, but you'd have to ask one of the brothers to be sure. Hell, Devon works for the police department up there when they have a rough case, why anyone would believe they'd let a killer work with the department is beyond me."

Courtney's eyes fluttered open. "I've got to go, she's awake. Let me know if Tex finds out anything." He ended the call, with a brief thought to the youngest Alpha, Tex. Unlike most Alphas, Tex didn't have to fight for his position, he took over the remaining members of his former clan when they killed Avery, the previous abusive Alpha. Tex had his work cut out for him to get the clan back on the right track and heal the damage Avery had done.

"How long have you guys been up?" she asked, adjusting so she could look at him.

"Not long. I got a call that woke us."

"Now that you're off the phone, why don't you come back?" She patted the blanket, inviting him to join her.

"That's an offer I can't refuse." He slid off the sofa and onto his knees next to her. She rose off her elbow, coming closer to her, while the fireplace cast a warm glow around her, making her look angelic. His beast rubbed along the edges of his skin, the desire for his mate growing stronger. "You're beautiful." A warm blush spread across her cheeks like a brush fire.

She tugged a hand through her hair. "I'm sure I look a mess. My hair…"

He pressed his lips to hers. The sweet kiss to show her how he felt turned passionate as the desire pulled closer to the surface. Sliding his tongue between her lips, he explored the contours of her mouth. The sweet taste of her pulled him farther in. Drawing his hand through her hair, he kissed her deeper, drinking her down as if he couldn't get enough of her. When he finally broke the kiss, they were both breathless.

"Where's Tad?"

"I kiss you like that and your mind is on another man. If the three of us weren't mated, I'd be jealous." He kept his tone low and playful, making it clear he was only joking.

"She doesn't want me to miss the fun."

Milo turned to see Tad standing in the doorway, his clothes wet from being outside.

"Both of you are all I've thought about since we first touched," Courtney admitted, her skin flushed. "The surge of power that flowed through us must have done something to me, because I can't think of anything else right now. I don't understand what's happening, or why…but I want you both…now." She held out her hand to Tad.

He kicked off his shoes and tugged off his shirt before accepting her hand.

"What are you saying, Courtney?"

* * *

She took a deep breath and pushed her fears aside. No longer would she deny her body what it craved, not when her future was looking so bleak.

"I thought it was clear. I want you. Take my mind off everything else, relieve this burning desire within me." With one hand still in Tad's, she used her other hand to reach out and grab hold of Milo's shirt. "This is so unlike me, but I can't control this. I need you both."

Milo wasted no time stripping his clothes off, and she suspected he was also overcome by yearning. Naked, he crawled onto the makeshift bed next to her and tugged her shirt up over her head.

Instinctively, she drew her hands up to cover her nakedness, but he stopped her.

"Don't. I want to see all of you. You're beautiful."

Tad nodded. "I thought the same thing when I pulled you from your car. You stole all logical thought when I first saw you."

She wanted to deny it; she didn't see herself the way they did. She was a full figure woman, with curves in all the areas many women despised. As a journalist she was always busy chasing down a story, even worked out a few times a week to keep in shape just in case, but it never surpassed her love of baking and sweets. Thoughts of her appearance were pushed away when Tad stepped toward them.

He tugged off his wet jeans before joining them on the other side of her, then claimed her mouth. She moaned around Tad's unrelenting kiss. For a brief moment she felt a twinge of jealousy from Milo but it passed quickly, to be replaced with the knowledge there was enough of her for both of them.

Milo pushed her bra to the side as his lips feverishly claimed her nipple. His other hand went to the waistband of her yoga pants, pushing them down her legs. With them went her last shred of reservation.

"Please…" She reached out, her hand landing firmly on Milo's chest, forcing him closer to her. Milo's shaft pressed tight against her thigh. They had her captive between their bodies, making her feel safe and wanted.

Milo's fingers slipped between her legs and teased her bundle of nerves, dragging pleasure from her in hard, hot waves. She moaned around Tad's unrelenting kiss. Milo's fingers thrust into her as his thumb continued to wring more pleasure from her core.

Tad's teeth grazed her lower lip and he pulled back enough to let her cries of frustration escape.

"I need one of you inside me. Please…" They stopped, sharing a glance before Milo slipped on top of her, angling between her spread thighs. He hovered above her, his shaft teasing along her entrance without entering as he watched her. Waiting, he gave her another moment to change her mind before his desire took his last shred of control and he drove into her with one powerful thrust. He gave her no time to catch her breath before he began rocking in and out.

Tad scooted from behind and knelt before her, his hard length jutting toward her. Without invitation, she took him into her mouth, working her way to the base. She used her hand to cup the end of the hard shaft, moving her mouth up and down the length, slowly at the tip. Tad groaned and reached to cup the back of her head. He allowed her to set the pace.

Trapped in the tempo of Tad's thrusts, she fought to find the perfect cadence to allow them to work together. Their rhythm quickly synced and she moaned, knowing they were being pleasured as one, rocking together in perfect harmony, as her ecstasy began to overwhelm her. Digging her nails into the back of Tad's thighs, she held on to him as every pump sent pulses exploding through her. She came apart at the seams, her inner muscles clenching around Milo as he continued to drive his shaft into her.

Rapture engulfed her. Tad cried out his release. She writhed beneath Milo, swallowing Tad's juices, before another wild climax spiraled through her. Milo cried out as he slammed home a final time before he collapsed next to her, their legs still entangled.

Tad slipped from her lips and leaned against the sofa, his eyes closed. She tugged his hand, still reeling. He scooted down to lay next to her.

Eventually her breathing returned to normal, and she cuddled against both of her mates, contented. She let the thought of mates play through her mind. It was so completely different than what she'd searched for all her life, but it seemed to be just what she never knew she needed.

Chapter Six

Tad rested his head next to her, his arm wrapped across her waist holding her tight against him. Milo laid just on the other side of her, his arm just below Tad's, his fingers brushing against both of them. It seemed so peaceful, like this was how it was always supposed to be. For that brief time, he was able to forget just what he found outside, and live in the moment with his mates.

"I hate to spoil this moment." Milo propped himself up on his elbow.

"But?" Courtney asked.

"You need to know that it's believed Jeffery is in Alaska. Supposedly there's an eyewitness that saw him boarding a plane headed for Seattle. The plane never made it there or anywhere as far as we can tell. We have people looking, and Tex is following up on any possible leads in Texas."

Tad met Milo's gaze, just as everything clicked into place in Tad's mind. "That explains what I smelled outside."

"What?" Courtney started to move but their embraces kept her snugly between them.

"This house is set far enough away from the road and town that you don't get unwanted visitors, especially in a storm like this. The only scents I should have smelled besides ours is Hazel and Tate's. That wasn't the case, there was at least one addition scent. It was an animal, not a shifter, but it was near a human recently." Tad raised his arm to draw a finger over her cheek. "We'll keep you safe. When Jeffery decides to make himself known, we will be ready."

"Quinn is also on his way so he can be one of the first planes in when the weather clears." Milo laid his head next to her, breathing deep. "Your fear, it's different. Not as powerful as before."

She sighed. "I'm tired. Tired of running from him. He's killed before and I know he'll do it again given the chance, but honestly I'm just tired of it all. My life has been hell since I went to the police. If it's all going to come to an end, even if it means my life…then so be it. I just want it over with. After all *that*, there's no better way to end life."

"We're going to have a lot more of *that* in the future. Nothing is going to happen to you, so don't talk like that." Milo nuzzled against her.

"He's right, things are going to be fine. I'm going to call my family and see if my brothers, Turi and Trey, can make it off the island. If they can, they should be able to make it here in bear form without any issues. The twins are second to the youngest but since the rest of us are assisting the Alaskan Tigers, they're on the island managing our sleuth with my father, Devon." He brought her and

Milo's hands together in his. "We're mates, and I'll be damned if I'm going to let anything divide us."

"I can't have you risk your brothers for me."

"There's no risk. I told you shifters are nearly impossible to kill, and all of us, including the twins, are trained for this. We know the threats against our kind from a young age, and almost from the time we can walk we're trained to protect ourselves and our kind." Courtney's fear might've been gone for the moment, but Tad's anger was rising to an all time level. If he got his hands on Jeffery, he'd kill him just for terrifying Courtney. The need to protect a mate rose above all else.

Unlike the tigers, Tad's sleuth wasn't as strict about protecting their home. Since they were surrounded by water on all sides, and only family members lived on the island, they hardly needed to worry about it. Until the Alaskan Tigers and Kodiak Bears joined forces, the Browns pretty much stayed out of things, keeping to their island. When bears mated, they rarely had feelings of divided loyalties between their clan and their mates like some other shifter groups did.

"I'll make breakfast while Tad calls his brothers." Milo leaned into her, kissing her briefly before standing up and grabbing his clothes as he left.

Tad admired Milo for being strong enough to walk away from Courtney. He wanted nothing more than to snuggle against her body until he could make love to her again. Almost as if by command his shaft hardened, forcing a groan from him. Oh, how he wanted her again.

She turned to him, sliding her hand down his body. "I'm ready again if you are."

"Oh, darling..." He claimed her mouth as she wrapped her fingers around his shaft. Sucking her bottom lip into his mouth, he lightly ran his teeth over it before letting it go. "There's no doubt that I'm ready, but your safety is more important. I need to call Turi and Trey." He forced himself to move away from her and grab his jeans. Slipping them back on, he found they had dried some by the fire while he was otherwise engaged.

"Spoil sport." She tugged the blanket around her body, covering up her nakedness. Humans were never as comfortable about their naked bodies as shifters.

"Here." He tossed his shirt to her since he didn't see hers anywhere in sight. "The hot water is hooked up to the generator if you want to take a shower."

"That would be perfect. I cleaned most of the soot and dirt from the fire off in a gas station, but a real shower would make me feel better." She slipped his shirt over her head and stood. "Care to join me?"

His bear roared within in, demanding he join her. "I'll take a rain check until there's enough hot water that we don't risk standing under a cold shower." With a quick nod she left him standing there, watching her hips sashay away from him. Itching to follow her, he forced himself to pick up the phone and call his brothers.

* * *

Bacon sizzled in the skillet, pancake batter sat to the side waiting to be put on the griddle, and Milo was cracking eggs for omelets when Tad came into the kitchen. The connection between Tad and him had been a little surprising. He remembered Taber and Thorben had mentioned being able to feel each other's emotions, and they knew each other's next moves. Some of that was because they were twins, and the rest came from mating with Kallie, but there was no other connection between them.

Milo felt drawn to Tad, not in the same way as Courtney, but in a deep almost loving way. The love between them was strong, sharing the common bond of their mating with Courtney, even if their relationship wasn't sexual.

Tad leaned against the counter, his brow furrowed in thought. "I've spoke with Turi. Trey's out dealing with a few things because Dad's off the island. With Dad gone, he's staying, but Turi will be here within the hour."

"There's more, isn't there? I can feel it."

"There was blood in the air when I was outside…and this." Tad pulled a piece of cloth from his pocket and laid it on the counter. Blood soaked the beige material. "It's not his, there's a different scent to it. A call came through for a search party…a plane had a rough landing in a field not a quarter of a mile from here. If I had to guess, the blood would match the pilot. We can add another body to Jeffery's count."

"Devon's been searching for the plane Jeffery was seen boarding. It's going to lead him straight to Jeffery and us." Milo frowned, tossed the last eggshell in the trash, and washed his hands. "Is there any way to let Devon know who they're up against in case they find him before we do?" From what Courtney said, there was no doubt Jeffery would kill again. He wouldn't go down without a fight.

"Turi's going to try to find him before heading for us. In the meantime we need to be ready. We're sitting ducks if they come after him here. Being on the hill provides us a little advantage but I'm going to call Hazel and Tate and get them over here with an assault rifle or shotgun. Our handguns won't take him out long distance if we need to save any of the search team."

"We're going to have to tell Courtney."

Tad poured a cup of the coffee Milo had brewed and nodded. "I'll do it, and then I'll call Tate. I'll also have Hazel prepare something if we need to wipe the memories of the search team or police. Will you update Ty and Quinn?"

"Yeah." Milo flipped the bacon before looking back at Tad. "She can do that?"

"She's an exceptional witch."

"It's a skill my clan could benefit from. Do you think she would be interested in teaming with us occasionally?"

"She prefers her privacy here, but I believe she would be willing as long as she was able to remain here. This is her home, where her son and husband are buried." Tad set the coffee aside. "Hazel took Tate in when he was just a cub. His family disappeared, leaving him behind. She's always had a special connection to shifters because of her abilities, so she claimed Tate as her son. She'll do what she can for our kind. She feels it's her duty for being given Tate. Before him, she was a mess, her family was killed in a fishing accident. Tate was her second chance, and she never took it for granted."

"If she isn't interested, I won't push her. Courtney is the most important thing right now, and any help they'll give us will be appreciated." Milo grabbed the tongs and pulled the bacon from the skillet, placing it on a plate with paper towels. "I'll make the calls, then finish breakfast."

"Easy for you, I've got the hard part…telling Courtney."

Milo let out a deep laugh and set the plate of bacon aside. "I don't envy you there. She's a strong woman, but it might be enough to bring that fear back. No matter what she said this morning, she's not willing to give up her fight. She'll bring Jeffery down if she can do it. Though I'd prefer we do it, and save her the trouble of a trial."

"A man like Jeffery has connections. As long as he's alive, he's a threat to her. The only way to eliminate the threat is to eliminate him. If he's out of the picture, he can't order a hit on her or anyone else."

"Then that's settled. Let's just keep it from her and Quinn for now. I don't believe Courtney would agree with our stance, and I know for damn sure Quinn won't. If he thought as a shifter, he would…but being raised without any of our kind around him, completely in the human world, he thinks too much like them."

They shared a brief look, letting each other know they were on the same page. Then Tad made his way back to the bedroom where Courtney was showering.

With the thought of calling his Alpha, Milo rolled his shoulder to check the progress it was making. In just twenty-four hours, his shoulder was already nearly healed, or at least as healed as it would ever be. He considered the fact that within the next forty-eight hours the blizzard would pass and the airport would reopen. He was expected to return to the compound. The time was limited for them to convince Courtney she needed to go with them.

No wonder some of the shifters envied the Kodiak Bears and other less organized groups. They didn't have the same division of loyalties the Alaskan Tigers went through. They never had to choose between their mate or their clan or have to balance the two. Milo was one of the Elders guards, but he wasn't as high ranking as Felix and Adam were. Somehow, they still managed to balance their mates and their duty to the clan. Hopefully, Milo would be able to find that same balance.

Chapter Seven

Courtney sat surrounded by more men than she ever been around at once. As a journalist, she worked alone and rarely had to go into the office; all of her assignments were emailed in. She had lived a life of near solitude. Milo and Tad were on either side of her, and Tad's hand was on her thigh while Milo had his around her shoulders. Their touch calmed her, kept her focused on what they were discussing.

Turi, Hazel, and Tate sat across from her. Turi was so much like Tad except his hair was a lighter brown, and full of sun kissed highlights; he put her at ease. Hazel made her uncomfortable. She was too silent, as if she knew something was coming but wouldn't say it aloud. Did she know something the others didn't? Could she see the future?

Tate sat there quietly, his dark eyes watching intently. His shoulder length hair was silver. Not gray, but shiny like sterling silver, highlights that sparkled when the light hit it. The flannel shirt and jeans added a country appearance to his otherwise unusual looks.

"Dad is going to search this way," Turi said. "Hopefully if Jeffery gets this far, Dad can detour the police and search team until we're able to deal with the situation. Then we won't have to erase their memories." He grabbed another muffin off the tray Milo had provided.

"If things can be avoided, I prefer it." Hazel rose from her seat. "Messing with someone's memories is something I'd rather not do. But to keep us safe, I'll do whatever is needed. I'll be ready if and when you need me. If you'll excuse me, I need to prepare."

Tad nodded. "If you go down the hall to the second door on the right, that's Lisa's study. I have a fire going in there for you, it should be warm enough now. Please let us know if you need anything."

"Thank you." She disappeared down the hall.

"Please excuse my mother, she's usually more friendly," Tate said once Hazel was out of hearing range. "She's focused on trying to sense what's going to happen. She'll give us whatever warning she can before he gets here. The ritual to remove someone's memories is demanding, so she'll need whatever time we have to prepare herself."

"There's no need to apologize. You're both doing me a huge favor. I'll be in your debt." Tad's voice was clear and full of authority, but there was also a softness to it, conveying just how thankful he was for their help.

Tate shook his head, his silver hair sliding forward. "You know that's not how we are."

"I know, but that doesn't change anything. When you need anything, know the Kodiak Bears will be at your back."

"As well as the Alaskan Tigers," Milo added.

"Thank you." Tate smiled.

A few days ago, his smile would have made Courtney weak in the knees, but now that she had Tad and Milo she barely noticed. Nevertheless, she was sure he was a heartbreaker with the girls.

She couldn't offer her strength like Tad and Milo could, so she offered her talents instead. "I'm extremely grateful too, but in a fight…well, I doubt it needs to be said I wouldn't be much help. However, I'm one hell of a baker. If I make it out of this alive, you'll have an endless supply of sweets whenever you like."

"A baker? Tad, it looks like you've found the perfect mate." Tate chuckled, glancing at Courtney. "Tad's got the biggest sweet tooth of anyone I know, and that's saying something with my love of sweets. Not to mention his family is a bunch of hungry bears. You might have your hands full trying to keep him supplied, but I expect to at least get a sample from time to time…or I'll have to kill him for it."

"We've been down that road before, wolf. You, my friend, have the scars to prove it," Tad teased.

"Because you took a cheap shot." Tate rubbed his side.

"It will be nice to have others I can bake for," Courtney interjected. From how quickly the store bought muffins had disappeared, she suspected she'd be baking a lot. Thankfully, Milo could cook, which would allow them to split the duties and she wouldn't be in the kitchen from sun up to sun down trying to feed both of her hungry men.

The thought of splitting the duties with Milo made her realize she wanted to live. It was strange to think she had accepted Tad and Milo, but part of her couldn't stand the thought of being away from them. It had to be the mating they'd told her about, because the rational part of her knew it was too fast and told her to run for the hills.

Milo leaned close to her until she could feel his breath on her cheek. "You can bake for me anytime, sugar." He kissed her before she could say anything.

"I think you have more on your mind than just her baking." Tate laughed at his own joke.

"I'm just glad to see my older brother will be well cared for by mates who can cook. He's helpless in the kitchen." Turi smirked at Tad and popped another piece of the muffin in his mouth.

"I'm not helpless," Tad insisted.

"Not helpless, my ass." Turi and Tate both erupted into raucous laughter, and Milo chuckled.

"Don't worry, love, you've got your own talents." Wiggling her eyebrows, Courtney tried to let him know what she meant. She'd rather have Tad and Milo in her bed than in the kitchen.

The realization of what she had said hit her full force.

Love.

It was all happening so fast, but even though she'd deny it to anyone who asked, she was falling in love with them. Falling hard for both of them. What if something happened to them because of this mess with Jeffery? Just like that, her fear seeped back in. She didn't want to lose them.

"I'd like a moment with my…sister-in-law." Turi scooted his chair back from the table and stood.

Tad growled, but Courtney squeezed his hand and met Turi's gaze. "A bit presumptuous, aren't we?" she asked.

"I don't believe so. You've mated with Tad and Milo, I can smell their mark on you. That makes your family. A wedding is a human thing. Though some shifters, especially those with human mates, do have them. Now, may I have a moment alone with you?"

She nodded. Milo removed his arm from her shoulders, letting her stand, but Tad wouldn't let go.

"I'll only be gone a few minutes." She leaned down and gave him a quick peck before strolling out of the room with Turi hot on her tail.

For total privacy, she headed for her mother's bedroom. Being at the back of the house it would be the coldest room, but it was also the farthest away from the others. It was the best they could do for privacy without going outside, though shifter hearing meant they still would be able to hear whatever was said.

She took a moment to look at her mother's room. Nothing had changed in all the years she been gone. Even the same yellow and white comforter covered the bed, making the room bright even in the dead of winter when it was dark most of the time. A picture of her and her mother at her graduation sat on the nightstand. She longed to see her mother again. Was her mother protected? Did it even matter if Jeffery was in Nome?

She pushed the thoughts aside and turned to Turi as he shut the door behind them.

"What did you want to see me about?" she asked.

He stood there, his hands in the pockets of his jeans, just staring at her as if he wasn't sure where to begin.

"My bother…he's a little…let's say over the top. Especially when it comes to the protection of women and children. As his mate you're going to get hit hard with that and I reckon very soon. I wanted a moment to ask that you give him leeway. He'll do it so he doesn't lose you as he lost…"

"Turi!" Tad bellowed. Loud footsteps could be heard in the hall seconds before the door flew open to reveal a very angry Tad. His fingers wrapped around Turi's neck and pushed him against the wall. "You have no right."

Seconds passed while she stood there in shock. "Tad…" She started to go toward him, her arm outstretched to touch him, but thought better of it at the last second. The anger poured off him in hot waves. If she touched him, it could easily be turned onto her. Instead she moved around him, leaning against the wall next to Turi's body so she could look Tad in the eye and put as much authority in her voice as she could muster.

"Stop. This is not the time to be fighting amongst ourselves."

"He had no right to mention Rosemarie." Even as Tad spoke she could see his grip relax.

Turi didn't fight or even move, he just stood pressed against the wall and waited for his brother to calm down. "With what's happening, she needs to know. She can't be expected to follow your overprotective orders if she doesn't completely understand. Are you willing to risk the safety of your mates because you're stubborn?"

"Stop this, both of you. This is insane." Courtney was hurt he hadn't trusted her enough to tell her about this Rosemarie, and that Turi had tried to. It was irrational since there had to be plenty of things she didn't know about him, just as he didn't know things about her. For Turi to risk his brother's anger, this had to be worth it.

She turned away. If they were going to fight it out and see who won, she wasn't willing to watch. She hadn't heard anyone come down the hall, but Milo was standing in the doorway appearing confused.

So I'm not the only one being kept in the dark.

It made her feel better about the situation for a moment, especially when Milo held out his hand to her. She went to him, pressing herself against his chest, comforted by the warmth of his embrace as he wrapped his arms around her. The only thing missing was Tad's touch to complete the trio.

Milo ran his hand down her back. "Courtney's right, Tad, this isn't the time for this. We can't fight amongst ourselves when there's danger lurking nearby. If there's one thing I know about Turi, he wouldn't risk your anger if he wasn't adamant it was for the best."

"Rosemarie has nothing to do with what is at hand." Tad growled.

Turi didn't back down. "She has everything to do with it when your decisions to protect your mates will be affected by what happened in the past. If Courtney knows, she might listen to you instead of reacting to the orders you give. She hasn't been raised among us and she doesn't understand the danger. If she questions your order because she feels you're just being an overprotective ass, she might get hurt...or worse. Is that what you want?"

"If I was more protective, Rosemarie would still be alive." Tad released his grip on Turi's neck and stepped back.

"Rosemarie was a strong woman, and she refused to bend to any man's will. She wouldn't have listened to you unless she believed it was the right thing. Even if you had known what she was planning, you would have had to sedate her to stop her."

"What do you know, you were just a cub."

"I know it wasn't your fault. In the last few months with the Alaskan Tigers relying on you, you've begun to trust your instincts again. Now you need to stop blaming yourself. The first step to putting this behind you is telling your mates." Turi took a deep breath and let it out slowly. "You've always been stubborn, but now that you're mated you need to think about the large picture. I'll let the three of you work it out while I check the perimeter."

Milo stepped to the side of the doorway, taking Courtney with him so Turi could get around them, before shutting the door behind them.

"Courtney, turn on your mom's radio and find a station with white noise."

"Why?"

"It will make it harder for anyone else to hear whatever Tad needs to get off his chest. There's no need for Tate or Hazel to hear it." Milo kissed her forehead before she did as he asked.

"They already know." Sadness choked Tad's voice. "Rosemarie…"

Two for Protection: Alaskan Tigers

Chapter Eight

Tad sank down on the bed, lost in his thoughts. The day was playing out in his mind as if reliving it again, the terror, anger, and heartache tearing off the scab over the wound. It was so realistic he could smell her perfume, only to be replaced by the sickening smell of blood. Rosemarie's blood.

After flipping on the radio by the bed, Courtney came to him, gently placing her hand over his. "Whenever you're ready." She was so patient and understanding. He didn't deserve her.

He met her gaze. The fear of not being able to protect her ate at him, tearing away his confidence. No wonder fate decided she needed two mates. He had already proven once he couldn't protect those around him. At least she'd have Milo by her side if he failed her.

Milo came to stand in front of them and leaned against the dresser. "Whatever happened, nothing is going to change our mating. We'll need to find a way to work through it. I've always believed it would help to move past what's bothering you if you talk to someone. Talk to us."

Tad forced himself to begin. "For my family, males have always overrun the population, and females are rare. When one is born they are cherished, protected, and sheltered. It was no different for my cousin, Rosemarie. As my aunt's third child, she was only a year younger than me, and we were close. So close that when I went through the change at fifteen, it brought on hers. Shifting early brought changes to her, and she was more irritable about being contained. She saw it as unfair that the males could do as they pleased. Being surrounded by everyone all day, I needed space at night, so I would slip out of the house after everyone was asleep and wander the island in my bear form. It was so peaceful then." He looked up at Milo, knowing if anyone understood it would be him. Milo had also grown up surrounded by his clan, but he enjoyed his time alone. It was what provoked him to venture off on his own for a time.

"Rosemarie slipped out and followed me. There were trespassers on the island that I was sniffing out. Wanting to confront them when I located them, I stayed human. I was nearing the poachers when I realized she was there. Her scent permeated the island, as does all of the family, so I never thought twice. Through the trees, I could see them, and they were focused on her. She was unaware of the danger she was in, roaming through the woods without a care in the world. The island was supposed to be safe, she never…"

"Tad…" Courtney squeezed his hand.

He closed his eyes, taking strength from her before shaking his head. "No, if I don't get this out now, I never will." They remained quiet, waiting for him. "I stepped out of the woods, hoping to pull their attention from her. Instead, it only made things worse. They shot, bullets sliced through her, blood squirted through the air. She should have been able to heal the shots, but the youngest one jerked when he saw me, sending his shot too high…hitting her in the head. She was dead before she hit the ground."

"Oh, love." The sympathy in Courtney's voice pained him. He didn't deserve it, not when he was the cause of his cousin's death.

Standing, he pulled away from her and stalked to the window. "She was killed because I wasn't on my game. Her blood is on my hands as much as if I pulled the trigger myself."

"You were young, alone, and there was nothing you could have done to stop them," Milo said. "It isn't your fault. I'm sure no one blames you." The floor creaked under his weight as he stepped away from the dresser and neared Tad.

"I couldn't protect Rosemarie. How am I supposed to protect my mates?" Losing either of them would be unbearable, especially if it was his fault. In that instant, he realized it wasn't just about protecting Courtney, but also about protecting Milo.

"Tad, you've been in the role of protector all your life. You've stood for those who couldn't do for themselves, you jumped when the Alaskan Tigers needed back up, you saved countless lives, not to mention the ones you've made better by just there. You're not responsible for the actions of others."

Courtney placed her hand on his arm, drawing his gaze from the window. "You can't beat yourself up for it, you're not to blame."

"How do you know?" Tad glanced at Courtney. "You've just met me, and fate announces we're destined to be together. How can you believe I'm worthy of you?"

"You can tell a lot about a person in a relatively short time. I know you're a good person, and you wouldn't put anyone in harm's way if you could avoid it." She moved enough to place her body between him and the window, wrapping her arm as much as she could around his waist.

"She's right." Milo joined them, placing his hand on Courtney's back and the other on Tad's shoulder. "I've known you for a few years, and time and time again you've proved yourself worthy. I'd cover your six in a battle any day."

From Milo, that was high praise. He wouldn't just follow anyone's lead. When he was coming of age, he'd spent a few years off by himself before joining the Alaskan Tigers because he didn't want to get into the politics of a clan. When Ty became the Alpha, Milo dedicated himself to the clan as one of the Elder guards. He was now assigned to Bethany's protection, but occasionally assisted with Tabitha's.

"We're a team, we'll protect each other." Milo squeezed Tad's shoulder. "Nothing's going to happen to Courtney or any of us."

"I hope so," Tad whispered. Pulling them both tight against him, sorrow filled his chest making it hard to breath, as if he had already lost one of them.

Courtney wrapped her arm around Milo, completing the connection between them. "You mentioned Tate and Hazel already knew. How?"

"They were visiting the island at the time. It's when we found out about Hazel's ability to remove memories from humans. It's what saved them, that and Dad."

"If a shifter is killed in their animal form, they revert back. The poachers would have seen it happen. It can also happen when a shifter is gravely injured and can't hold onto their beast," Milo explained as Courtney's confusion tingled along the lines of their bond.

"Dad is the leader of the sleuth. He forbade us from killing them." Unable to stop himself, Tad's embrace tightened around them. "Rosemarie's murderer got away without the knowledge he killed someone."

"What would the knowledge have done? It wouldn't have made anything better. Instead it would have put your sleuth and our kind at risk. That wouldn't bring justice for Rosemarie. Only more death." Milo pushed Tad to see the truth.

"Doing nothing brought no justice to Rosemarie. She deserved more from me, from everyone."

"We've both seen more than our fair share of blood and death. No matter what happens it can never bring back someone who was killed. Do you really think justice is ever served?"

Milo might have had a point, though it didn't change the guilt Tad carried when he thought of that night. Rosemarie looked up to him. He should have protected her, and in the end he failed her. Somehow he had to prove himself worthy of Courtney and Milo, even if it was the last thing he did.

"Tad." Courtney cupped his cheek, and waited a heartbeat before continuing. "What happened to Rosemarie is awful, and I'm truly sorry, but you can't blame yourself. From the stories you and Milo shared last night, you've proved yourself as honorable. Nothing we can say or do will bring back Rosemarie, nor will it take away the pain. You'll have to move on, past what happened, without basing every decision you make on that night. No one blames you for what happened, and you shouldn't either."

He rubbed his face along her palm, kissing the bend of her wrist as he did so. His beast demanded the comforting touch, refusing to let him pull away from her. "You weren't there when it happened."

"I've been to Kodiak Bear's Island and I've never seen it," Milo said. "Devon, Ava, your brothers, none of them blame you."

"Have you ever been to the island when I'm not there? Notice that Aunt Bev is around? She keeps her distance when I'm there. She blames me…damn it, Rosemarie was her only daughter. I can't fault her for it either." Tad wanted the conversation over. He was tired of living in that day so many years ago. "It's my past Turi felt the need to bring to light again. There's no need for either of you to suffer due to my mistakes."

Milo shook his head. "Each of our pasts affects our future. We are no longer three individuals living their own lives. We're joined together as mates, and that makes us one." His cell rang, forcing him to take his arm away from Courtney and unclip it from his belt. "It's Tex." Milo stepped away to take the call.

Coming out of the memories, Tad moved them away from the window, not wanting to put Courtney in any more danger. He hugged her against him, resting his head on top of her and just breathing her in. His mate, the woman he was destined to be with, to share with Milo. Even after hearing the worst of his past, she didn't turn from him. When she could have sought comfort in Milo's arms, she didn't. She embraced them both, as they both tried to get him to see the light. It was more than he deserved.

"I know you're still angry with Turi, but he was right. I trust you and Milo. My rational side says it's all too fast and that I shouldn't, but the connection I feel between us is stronger than anything else. It wins out. I know you'll both keep me safe at all costs. Don't let bringing this up make you doubt yourself. Jeffery is dangerous. We all have to be on our toes if we're going to make it through this alive."

"We're going to be fine, and this will all be behind us soon. Then we can move on with our lives together."

He closed his eyes and just enjoyed the mixture of emotions that coursed through him. So much was going on within in, but the strongest of it all was the unending love for both his mates. When he thought of Milo, he wished he was there and longed for his touch to complete them.

* * *

The house was quiet as Milo made his way down the hall, giving Tad and Courtney privacy while he took the call from Tex. Hopefully, while he was busy with the call, she would make progress with Tad. They didn't have the manpower for the best warrior among them to be questioning himself. In order to keep Courtney safe, Tad had to be at his best. That meant moving past what happened to Rosemarie.

"Hey, Tex, what did you find?"

"Actually, not a lot. The apartment is immaculate. I believe it's a decoy. Connor's searching property records for anything else in his name or that's linked to him. I've spoken to the witness, and she even pointed Jeffery out from a photo line up."

"But..." Milo pressed.

Tex remained silent for another moment before answering. "His business partner was found dead this morning. They're looking at Jeffery for it. Without the partner flipping on him for a lighter sentence, probation, it puts the case on shakier ground even with Courtney's testimony. His lawyers are all over the news saying the partner framed him, stole his DNA and everything. If he knocks them both off, the case is over."

"Shit. The more blood he has on his hands, the easier the kills become." Milo opened the curtain enough that he could look out on the grounds without giving anyone that might there a clear shot. Turi and Tate were just coming around the house, making their pass along the perimeter.

"Any sign of the weather breaking? Maybe you guys can get back to the compound," Tex suggested.

"Not going to happen right now. We have things lined up for Taber to fly in and get us at the slightest break in the storm, but this weather is just too nasty to fly in. Too much ice mixed in with the snow, not to mention the visibility is no more than fifty feet. I won't risk him trying to fly in these conditions. If he's going to come after her, we'll be ready." His tiger itched for a fight.

Taking Avery out of his position of power over the Texas clan had reminded Milo just how much his beast enjoyed the action. It felt good to be back in the fight, protecting his clan. Since his shoulder injury, he had been out of the action, stuck on the compound grounds on home protection for too long. Now things had changed, and his beast enjoyed it. This bastard would suffer for threatening his mate. No harm would come to Courtney while he was alive.

"I'll be in touch if I learn anything else. We're just a call away if you need anything."

"Thanks. Turi, Tate, and Hazel are here so we're ready if Jeffery wants to take his shot at her."

He ended the call and clipped his cell back on his jeans, still scanning the grounds. Nothing seemed out of the ordinary. Still, he had a feeling it wouldn't be long before things weren't so calm. The thought sent his fingers twitching along the butt of his gun.

The whole situation bothered him. There was something about Jeffery Park that didn't make sense. He had a house that was only for show. That didn't fit with a drug smuggler; he should have been living it up. So where was he normally? Not at the mansion that was on record, that was for sure.

Tad's laptop sat on the table. With nothing to do other than wait for Jeffery to show himself, Milo decided to see what he could find.

Connor might be the geek of the clan, but Milo had his own abilities when it came to finding information. Those years spent away from the clan left him with some very important contacts. Once he had some of the basic information, he'd make a few calls. Within a few hours, he was sure he'd know whatever Jeffery was trying to hide.

Chapter Nine

As he stood in the shadows of the porch, Tad waited while Turi did the final pass of the perimeter for the night. He had been trying to get Turi alone all evening. Instead, his brother always seemed to sidestep out of it. Not this time. It was time for them to have a few words, though what those words would be he wasn't completely sure. Part of him wanted to scream at Turi for bringing up what happened to Rosemarie, while the other side knew without Turi's blunder the events of the day would have stayed locked away in the dark place within him.

Turi stepped onto the porch, shaking the snow from his shoulders and hair before looking over at Tad. "What are you doing out here? I thought you'd be in there snuggling with your mates. Oh, how the older Brown brothers have fallen." He teased.

Tad couldn't help but smile since. The eldest two brothers were mated and were just as Turi described them. They couldn't get enough of their mates. Taber and Thorben were completely at Kallie's beck and call. Not that he had any room to talk. In just a short time, Courtney already had him wrapped around her little finger.

"Boy, one day you'll be mated and you'll be the same way."

"Not me." Turi sounded certain, as if he had a say in it. "Not going to happen, especially if Mom's right. There's no way Trey and I could share a woman like Taber and Thorben do. We fight over stupid shit too much. Plus, Trey is too possessive."

The youngest set of twins were a handful, especially when they were growing up. Now that they were older, they were starting to calm down. Even with the occasional teasing, they were as close as any of them. Actually, now that Tad thought about it, Turi and Trey were closer than even Taber and Thorben.

"Once you've found your destined mate, nothing can stop you from claiming her, not even the idea of sharing her with Trey." He couldn't help but chuckle at the idea. The poor woman who had to deal with them day in and day out deserved a medal. "About earlier…"

Turi held up his hands and cut him off. "I know you're pissed but they deserved to know, especially Courtney. Mom always said you have to go into the mating with no secrets."

"It wasn't your secret to tell."

"That might be true, but you weren't going to do it. No one else was here who would do it. Tate and Hazel might know, but they would never say anything. Hazel might have adopted Tate and accepted some of the shifter ways, but she doesn't understand mating. She doesn't realize the undeniable draw to your mate, the need to be with her. So she couldn't understand the need to be completely honest either."

Tad ran his hand through his hair, shaking off the snow. "For someone who isn't mated and doesn't want to be, you sure understand the connection."

"You said it yourself, there's nothing like it and there's no way to deny it. Keeping something that made you the man you are a secret will only lead to problems. Courtney might be taking this well right now, even accepting there are shifters, but you start lying, even by omission, and it's not going to go over well."

He wanted to punch his brother. She was *his* mate. Did being raised in the human world differ that much from how he was raised? His family was secretive, so much that the children barely left the island until they were adults and could keep their secret. Even then, only Devon ventured off for supplies, while the rest stayed on the island unless they began to get desperate to find their mate.

The brothers had duties to the Alaskan Tigers, and their kind. They traveled frequently to the Alaskan Tigers' compound, and on missions. They rarely had contact with humans who were unaware shifters lurked in the shadows, living their own lives. If he was honest with himself, he knew very little about the way humans were raised. It had never been important for him to find out until now.

Whatever differences he had from Courtney needed to be addressed before it caused problems in their mating. Milo had spent years among humans; surely he'd help Tad.

With no anger left within him, Tad let out a soft growl of frustration.

"All I'm saying is stop interfering with my mating, unless you want me to do it when the time comes for you."

"There's no reason for me to interfere any longer. Just remember she's been through a lot and you need to be straight with her. Lisa raised her right, and she has a good head on her shoulders. She'll keep herself safe. You need to focus on Jeffery if you want to eliminate the threat to her. If you watch over your shoulder to make sure she's not doing something stupid, you're going to get yourself killed. Losing one brother already this year was enough. I also don't want to drag your heavy body home and explain how you got your dumb ass killed to Mom." Without another word, Turi brushed past him and into the house.

Anger spewed forward, sending the bear within him close on its heels. He wanted to grab Turi by the neck. Turi might be an adult now but he wasn't too old for Tad to give him a lesson he wouldn't forget. Young bears needed to mind their elders if they wanted to live a long live. He threw his head back and let a deep growl escape, shaking the ground and sending snow falling from the trees. The beast within him wanted to shift, to run off the irritation at Turi. The only thing that stopped him was the sound of the door opening behind him.

"Stay inside, Turi, I've had enough right now."

"Courtney is worried about you. Your growl shook the whole damn house," Milo's deep voice called out. He never noticed before, but the sound of his voice was like echoing thunder. So much command and compassion held within those syllables.

He turned to find his mate alone. Movement by the window caught his gaze. Turi was doing his best to drag Courtney away from view, which only sent his beast growling again. No one should lay hands on her.

"Don't get upset with Turi, he's only doing as I asked," Milo said. "Courtney standing by the window makes her a target. Now if you get your ass inside, she wouldn't be fighting him. What the hell happened anyway?"

"Turi has always known how to get under my skin with his comments. I swear that boy needs put in his place and this time I'm about to do it. Taber and Thorben aren't here to protect his scrawny little ass this time." He looked back at the window. All was still, the curtain pulled tightly back into place.

"I don't believe this is the time for family fights. Our mate needs our support, she's beginning to climb the walls. In her mind, darkness only means one thing, that Jeffery will be on the move. His kind operates best at night. Darkness can hide him better from humans, making the police less like to catch him receiving the drugs. It does nothing for him when it comes to shifters. Still, if he's going to try to attack Courtney, tonight is his best chance. Tomorrow the storm will start to break up, and with a little luck Taber can fly in before the second one makes landfall."

"Go ahead inside, I need a few minutes first."

"No." Milo shook his head and stepped closer. "I promised Courtney I'd bring you back inside with me. She needs you, and I need to make a few calls. I spent the afternoon following up on this Jeffery Park. He's not who he says he is. There's a trail as long as I am tall of dead bodies in his wake. Drugs are his thing now because it's quick money, but he's no stranger to black market babies, human trafficking, whatever can bring him the thrill. Seems our mate got herself tangled up with a rather nasty fellow."

Tad rolled his shoulders and nodded. "I shouldn't have left you alone to deal with Courtney when I knew you were dealing with other things. Turi could have waited. Let's go put our mate's mind at ease." He made his way across the porch to the door with Milo a step behind him.

"She's our mate, we can cover for each other when one needs to deal with something, but right now she needs both of us as much as possible. She's scared, and though she is trying to hide it, being around so many strangers has her on edge. I don't believe it has anything to do with the fact all of us, except Hazel, are shifters."

"I know." He nodded and opened the door. Inside he found Tate stretched out on the sofa, his eyes closed. Turi was blocking the path between Courtney, who sat on the armchair, and the door.

"Get out of the way, Turi," Courtney demanded at the sight of her mates.

Tad shook off the snow that had gathered on his hair and shoulders and kicked off his boots. He was wet through from standing outside, but Courtney didn't seem to notice or care as she wrapped her arms around him.

"You're okay." She ran her hands over his back as if searching for injuries.

"I'm fine. What has you in such a state?" He focused on his mate, not giving Turi a second glance, his patience gone.

"Let's take this to the bedroom," Milo suggested. "You can change and we can have a little privacy." Without waiting for their response, he led the way down the hall.

"You both just want her to yourself, a little nooky before the fight," Tate hollered after them.

"You're jealous, Tate," Tad replied.

Tate's comment put ideas into Tad's head that made him want his mate naked under him. He wanted to feel himself buried deep within her as she took Milo in her mouth. The memory of that experience, with the glow of the fire dancing over their bodies, made him instantly hard.

"Doesn't sound like a bad idea to me," Courtney whispered.

Milo leaned against the door waiting for them, a cocky grin on his face. "It seems our mate is frisky."

As if on command, she tugged Tad's wet shirt from his jeans, pulling it up his chest and over his head. As quickly as it was done, her hands were back on his chest as she toyed with the little patch of hair between his pecs.

"I don't understand this need within me," she said, her voice husky. "It's always there, demanding the two of you. When you're beyond arm's reach, there's a longing that aches within me for your touch."

"Maybe this isn't the best time. We should wait until you're safe." Tad tried to reason with her before he lost whatever control remained. Her fingers teased along the waistband of his jeans, but it was her tongue flicking across his nipple that did him in. The need to throw her on the bed and claim her again took over logic.

"Now's the prefect time. If I'm going to die tonight I want to feel the two of you pressed against my naked body." Her breathy words came seconds before her hand dove inside his jeans.

"You're not going to die, none of us are, but we can give you what you want regardless." Milo came up behind them and kissed her neck.

Tad kicked the door shut and edged the trio closer to the bed. "My control is flimsy tonight, the beast within is on edge. I want you naked." He laced his fingers through her hair and forced her mouth closer to his.

He pressed his lips to hers, demanding her. His tongue dove into her mouth, teasing along hers in a hungry frenzy. He devoured her. The sweetness of the hot chocolate she had earlier still coated her mouth, making her even more desirable than ever.

Seconds before she tugged his jeans down his legs, he had enough logic left to grab his gun from the holster and place it on the bedside table. When she wrapped her fingers around the length of his shaft, it nearly stole his breath. Slowly she worked her way up and down the length of him. The passion controlling him didn't allow him to reconsider what they were doing. Danger might be lurking outside, but in that moment he didn't care. Turi, Tate, and Hazel would alert them. All that mattered right now were his mates.

"Naked," Milo urged. "I want her naked."

Tad gave her one final kiss before pulling back. The loss was immediate and his need for her came rushing back full force. Milo pulled her shirt over her head and Tad fumbled with her jeans.

"Let me." She quickly unbuttoned them and slid out of them, along with her panties, before glancing back at Milo. "If we're naked, then you should be too." She turned to him, her fingers unbuttoning his dress shirt while her other hand was firmly wrapped around Tad's shaft.

Milo slid his shoulder holster and gun off, setting it next to Tad's, before ripping his shirt off sending the remaining buttons flying through the air. "What?" He asked when they both looked at him. "Time is of the essence." He undid his jeans and stepped out of them, along with his boxers.

Courtney wrapped her free hand around his shaft. "Ahhh, two men standing at attention for me. I hope I don't let either of you down." She shot them a sexy grin that almost had Tad losing his patience.

"You couldn't, darling." Milo smiled and leaned in closer. He kissed a path down her neck. The sensations poured through the connection overwhelmed each of them as she became more aroused with each touch.

"On the bed," Tad ordered.

While Milo explored her breast, he wanted something a little farther south. She let go of their shafts and climbed onto the bed. Milo followed, quickly regaining his place kissing along her neck, slowly working his way back down to her breast. Tad stood there a moment, observing them. The way she came alive with their touch thrilled him. She was like a flower, waiting for that special moment to open up and let the whole world see how beautiful she was.

"Tad…" Her voice had such desire he couldn't deny her.

He slipped on top of her, his bulky frame hovering above her as he stared down at her, desire burning in her eyes. He teased along the curves of her hips, his fingers brushing against Milo. His shaft twitched with need, his bear clawed under his skin, impatient and demanding. He wanted to see the desire burn brighter in her eyes.

He blazed a hot, wet trail of kisses across her belly and stroked her thighs with his fingertips. With every touch, she arched her hips, demanding more. He loved that she couldn't get enough of him. Nudging her legs farther apart, his fingers delved inside her and she met the teasing thrusts. A demanding moan tore through the air.

Passion drove fire through him. Keeping his gaze on her, he slipped lower on the bed. The trail of wicked kisses tingled over her thighs. He moved his fingers until his thumb was lightly teasing over her bud before he replaced it with his mouth. Tiny nips and gentle licks flicked over her sweet spot until she wriggled beneath him. Her fingers locked in his hair, torn between pressing him closer and dragging him up.

"Tad!" She cried out, her legs twitching, and her back arching as the release he was waiting for found her.

"Yes, mate?"

"I want to feel you inside of me." Her voice was hoarse with need.

With another flick of the tongue over her sweet spot, he nodded. "Your wish is my command, mate."

He spread her legs farther, giving him the access he needed before filling her slowly, inch by inch. Halfway in, he slid out before thrusting back in, filling her completely with his manhood.

"Milo." She wrapped her hand around his shaft. "Now, please."

"This time is about you." He reclaimed her nipple, gently pulling it between his teeth.

Tad increased his pace, driving the force of each pump. The thrusts became deeper and faster, falling into a perfect rhythm, moving with precision. Her hand still worked down the length of Milo's shaft, keeping the connection between the trio burning.

Their bodies rocked back and forth, tension stretching Tad tighter as he fought to hold on until she came again. Tipping her head back, she cried out, her nails digging into his shoulder blades, arching her body into his. He pumped once more and shouted her name as his own orgasm followed.

Easing off of her, Milo quickly replaced him. Tad drew his hand through her hair, pulling it away from her face and kissing her deeply. He had wanted to taste her lips again since watching how they puckered as she came.

"Oh no, I want her to be able to scream my name just as she did yours." Milo shot them a quick smile before sliding his manhood inside her.

"I guess I'll have to give attention to the breast he neglected." Tad teased before kissing along her jawline to her neck. He loved the way her pulse sped up; her arousal was stronger to his bear nose just below her ear, making him want to bury his head there. Instead he continued down her chest until he reached her breast.

Kissing slowly around the nipple he watched his mates, he was surprised he felt no jealousy, only joy. Milo's hand left her hip, sliding up her body until it brushed against Tad's arm. The sensation of Milo's touch made Tad pause with his lips wrapped around Courtney's nipple.

For a moment he wasn't sure how to take the connection that sprang to life. It seemed to open more doors than just with Courtney. As it settled around him, he realized it was just another fold of the mating, allowing them the share the same bond they already had with Courtney. They would be in tune with each other's emotions at all times, not having to rely on her to be the middle that connected them. It would help in protecting Courtney from Jeffery.

With the connection easing through them, Courtney shouted Milo's name. Only to be followed seconds later by Milo's release. Milo slipped out of her and collapsed beside her. His gaze found Tad and they shared a knowing look. One that had Tad closing the distance between them and laying his hand over the other man's.

Eternity stretched on before their breathing returned to normal. They lay cuddled together, caressing each other with long, lazy strokes, enjoying the moment.

Two for Protection: Alaskan Tigers

Chapter Ten

Courtney and Tad strolled hand in hand back into the family room, while Milo stayed in the bedroom making calls. In that moment life was good. She didn't care that somewhere in the darkness Jeffery might be lurking, all she wanted was to be snuggled with her mates. Her body longed for Milo, but he'd promised he wouldn't be long.

"A little action to burn off some steam, huh, Tad?" Tate teased, munching on a bowl of popcorn.

"I've never known my brother to miss a moment." Turi chimed in.

"You won't disgrace a beautiful thing with your immature comments." Tad let go of her hand and pulled her into him. "Don't either of you have anything better to do?"

"Not me, I have plans to sit with the newest addition to our family. I have many stories of you I'm sure she's very interested in hearing."

"I think you've said enough." Tad glared at his brother; she could see he was trying to push the darkness away. It was clear the thoughts of Rosemarie were coming back to him.

She tapped her hand on his arm, and glanced to Turi. "I'm sure he has happier memories to share. Do you have any embarrassing moments you can tell me about?" A few amusing tales would help lighten the mood.

"I'm afraid now is not the time," Hazel announced. They turned to find her standing in the doorway.

"What is it, Mom?" Tate set the bowl of popcorn aside.

"They are nearing. If they continue, their arrival will be in twenty minutes. If they veer off the path, it'll be an hour."

"They?" Tad slid Courtney in front of him and wrapped his arms tightly around her.

"Your father and another man are on his tail. I don't believe they will catch him before he gets here. We need to be ready," Hazel explained.

"We'll be ready." Milo stated, coming to join them in the family room. "Courtney, I want you to stay in the study with Hazel. You'll be safe there and out of direct line if there's a firefight. The windows are too far off the ground for him to come in that way, leaving only one way."

"Turi, you're with the women," Tad ordered.

"Come on, bro." Turi complained.

Tad's body went stiff against her, and his fingers stopped teasing over her forearm. "You might be an ass, but you're still my brother. I want you safe and I need to know the women are protected. Two birds one stone, that kinda crap. Now I don't want to hear another complaint."

"Yes, sir." Turi quickly stood and saluted him before giving her a wink.

These two were enough to drive her insane. She couldn't imagine being surrounded by all six of the Brown brothers at once. How had their mother managed when they were young?

"Boys." Courtney intervened before Tad could do or say anything. She didn't need him beating the shit out of Turi. "Turi, you can use this time to give me the dirt on Tad."

"Come along with me, Turi," Hazel interjected. "There are a few things I'd like to do first and could use your help." She gave Tate a look that had him jumping to his feet.

"I'll come too."

"I believe they're giving us a private moment before the shit hits the fan." Courtney held her hand out to Milo. She wanted to feel them both pressed against her, to calm the storm that was wrecking havoc on her stomach. Anxiety and concern nearly overpowered her.

"Oh, darling." Milo joined them, wrapping his arms around both of them. "Everything is going to be fine." He nuzzled his head between the nook of her shoulder and Tad's chest.

"I brought him here, this isn't your fight. You shouldn't be risking yourselves to protect me. Damn it!"

"Courtney, you listen to me." Tad turned slightly so she could look at him without moving Milo. "We're not risking anything. I told you shifters are hard to kill. Nothing's going to happen to us. Dealing with Jeffery here on our terms will free you. You'll be able to live again without looking over your shoulder. This ends here and now."

"At what cost? When this is over, then what? How am I supposed to go back to my life in Texas? What about what has happened between us?" Questions poured off her tongue, and all she really wanted to hear was that things would be fine. That when things were finished with Jeffery, they would be there by her side. She had only known them a short time, but no longer could she picture her life without them.

"There's no cost, instead you'll gain your freedom back."

Milo nodded against her shoulder. "Nothing is going to change between us, we'll make this work. If you're unwilling to stay in Alaska, I'm sure Tex would be grateful for the support in Texas as he tries to put the pieces of his clan back together."

She let them hold her, to feel the truth of their words not just in her heart but in her mind as well. To stop thinking and to trust what she was feeling from them would take time. Right now, she forced the thoughts away.

"Things will work out." She said the words aloud to convince herself; they already seemed to know.

* * *

With their mate safe in the study, Milo knelt by the front window with Tad beside him while Tate covered the back of the house. The waiting game was the worst. He tried to relax to keep his shoulder lose when all the muscles wanted to do was contract. The dual ache forming between his shoulder blades let him know he was using his shoulder too much too soon. Tension of the muscles wasn't helping.

"The calls you made earlier, were you able to find out anything else on Jeffery? Anything we can use against him?"

He shook his head and glanced over at Tad. "The calls were for Ty. Seems the Minnesota Alpha isn't thrilled with the idea of Tabitha being able to have say over how he runs his clan. He wants the Queen of the Tigers to leave him and his people alone."

"What did Ty expect from you?"

"Calvin and I have some history. Ty thought I might be able to get through to him."

Tad's eyes widened with surprise. "Did you?"

Milo shook his head. "He's not willing to discuss all of his concerns over the phone but I'm making headway. I'll have to take a trip to Minnesota once we have Courtney safe. I was hoping the two of you would join me."

"A trip might be what Courtney needs." Tad smiled. The connection between them allowed Milo to know Tad was thinking more about getting their mate in bed again than actually seeing Minnesota. "That's if we can pry Lisa off her long enough. Lisa is pretty upset, since the two of them haven't spoken much in months. Their bond was weak because Courtney was trying to spread her wings. This event might be just what they need to reconnect."

Snow crunched, forcing their attention to return to the window. Just inside the perimeter, a man crouched by the tree line. If it wasn't for shifter vision, the man would have blended in almost perfectly.

"There he is," Milo said. Even with the distance, Jeffery's exhaustion was clear. He leaned against the tree, his chest rising and falling as he tried to catch his breath. In his condition he was no match for a strong man, let alone three shifters.

Tad brought his phone to his ear. "Dad, he's here." There was a brief pause before he replied. "Understood. Unless he makes a move, we'll stand down."

"Stand down?" Milo couldn't believe what he heard.

"Dad and Sheriff Lutz are coming up behind him now. We can't do anything until he's closer anyway, and we can't risk them getting hit by a stray bullet just to take him out."

"You're just going to let him live? Do you think a man like that will leave Courtney alone just because he's behind bars?" Milo was normally the calm one of the clan, willing to look at options other than eliminating the opposition. Not this time. This time he wanted Jeffery dead for his mate and for all the others he screwed with over the years, for the families of his victims.

"He'll die in prison. Locked up he won't be a threat to her."

"You honestly believe that? You can't believe he doesn't have someone else willing to do his dirty work. I'm not going to let this danger hang over her head just so you don't risk Devon's anger. This is our mate we're talking about." Milo stood, his gun in hand. He was determined to see the man pay. For the first time in his life he was truly bloodthirsty.

"You go out there with a gun with the search parties that close, and you're going to get yourself hurt or worse. How is that going to help her? Think about this, man." Tad turned to him. "Just see this play out. I guarantee he won't be alive long enough to cause any more problems for anyone."

"What do you mean?"

"Do you honestly think Devon is going to do nothing? The sheriff and his men, including my father, know who Jeffery is."

He moved back next to Tad, and glanced out the window. "Are you saying they'll kill him in cold blood?"

"No. I'm saying that Dad has ways of provoking him. Jeffery will make a move and there will be no other option." Tad nodded. "Watch."

"What if he doesn't?"

"Then we'll take care of him once the sheriff has him in custody. Poison in his food would make it look natural. There's no reason to bring attention to any of us."

"You've done this before?"

"When something has to be done, yes. We've never killed an innocent. I believe this is how some of those rumors of the Brown family being assassins started. Let's just say the previous generations methods weren't so unnoticeable." Tad must have seen Milo's surprise. He added, "This isn't any different then when your clan eliminated Victor. Protection of our kind and our mates is number one. You know that."

What Tad was suggesting teased along the lines of ethical, but when it came to protecting Courtney the lines weren't so black and white. The clan had done this before, protecting their own and their secret. This was no different.

Milo knelt back down by the window, watching as Devon's large frame came out of the trees. The Sheriff was just a step behind, his hand on his weapon. Golden blond hair stuck out from underneath police hat. His frame was a touch leaner than Devon's, but he was just as bulky. Both men were large and intimidating.

"Tad…the sheriff?"

"Lion shifter."

"Now I know why Devon works so well with him. Most would see his size and discount him on that. Another shifter wouldn't. What's a lion shifter doing in Alaska?"

"Hiding." Tad shot him a warning glance. "So keep it between us. Only Mom, Dad, and us boys know what Sheriff Leo Lutz is."

"Your family secrets are safe with me. Though I have to say it's nice to have the sheriff as one of us. Too bad the Fairbanks sheriff isn't a shifter," Milo joked.

The sheriff called out, and Milo wasn't sure what he said. Even with his superb hearing, he couldn't hear through glass. Only Jeffery's reaction as he spun around, his gun raised, let Milo know the fun was about to begin. If things got out of hand, he was glad Courtney was safe on the other side of the house.

Tad turned and whispered toward the kitchen. "Tate, join Turi with the women. Milo and I are going to assist the sheriff and my father." Without a complaint, Tate did as he was told and snuck away from where he'd been watching out the back window. They heard a door open and then shut.

"Let's go out the side. Move quickly, but keep to the shadows and stay out of Jeffery's sight." Tad stood, keeping his gun in hand, his gaze on the window. "He'll end this tonight by his own actions."

Milo hoped so; it would do a world of good for his mate to be able to put this whole thing behind her. Quinn would have to find another case to help make his career because this wouldn't be it. His mate was more important than his friend's career. One day, Quinn would understand.

Outside, wind rushed past him. Snow and ice hit him full force as they made their way toward what had turned into a shouting match.

"Drop the gun!" Devon's voice cut through the trees, sending Tad and Milo into overdrive.

Milo skid to a halt as loose snow flew through the air a few feet away from the scene. Jeffery had his gun pressed against Sheriff Lutz's temple, his eyes wide, desperation pouring from him. Milo aimed his gun, focusing on a kill shot.

"If you don't put down the gun you'll die here," Devon called out.

"You're alone and don't have a chance. I have the upper hand. Let me get what I came for and I'll be gone. No harm will come to him." Jeffery pressed the gun harder against Leo's head.

A headshot would kill even the most powerful shifter, yet Leo remained still. Everyone knew it would never come to that. It was just a way to get Jeffery off his game and give them a reason to end the man's life without looking like it was done in cold blood.

"I'm never alone." Devon nodded to Milo and Tad, who were both aiming at Jeffery.

Jeffery glanced over at them.

"Put the fucking gun down!" Tad hollered. The distraction gave Leo the opportunity he needed to jab his elbow into Jeffery's stomach and get out of the man's grip. The gun went off, hitting Devon in the shoulder. "Shit!"

Milo and Tad fired nearly simultaneously. Bullets cut through Jeffery's chest, sending him stumbling backward. Blood stained the snow red as he staggered back before falling.

"Devon, are you okay?" Milo asked as he covered Tad, who was checking Jeffery for a pulse.

"Bastard shot me." Devon bitched, his fingers instantly going to his shoulder. "Ava's going to be pissed I ruined another coat. Why don't they ever shoot you, Leo?"

"Guess I'm too quick for them." Leo teased. "You're just getting old, Devon."

"You're full of shit." Devon glared at Leo before turning to his son. "Is he dead?"

Tad nodded and holstered his gun. The muscles in his shoulders were tense with unspent energy.

They had been looking forward to a fight. Now it was over and the beasts within them refused to be sated. Milo slid his gun into his shoulder holster and looked to Leo. "Sheriff, I'd like to let Courtney know she's safe."

"Go ahead. You too, Tad. I'll need an official statement, but that can wait. Get back to your mate and let her know this is over. We'll be traipsing through Lisa's property for some time yet, but at least everyone's safe and no one shifted." Leo nodded to Devon. "You have to wait. With the others not far behind, you can't shift now. You'll have to let the medic attend to you and then you can go meet her."

"It would be better if no one got hurt," Devon complained, causing Tad to roll his eyes at his father before he started back to the house.

"Devon, you're worse than a woman. A little bullet wound won't kill you." Leo growled.

"Sadly enough, I don't feel relieved that it's over. I needed more action. That bastard should have suffered the terror he inflicted on her." Tad growled, stopping on his way to the house.

"I know the feeling. My beast wants to be let out. The important thing is she's safe. How about we burn this energy off with our mate?" Milo suggested.

"I can't think of anything better."

That idea seemed to please Tad. It sure did wonders for Milo.

Two for Protection: Alaskan Tigers

Chapter Eleven

Courtney sat by the fireplace in the study, her legs pulled under her as dread coursed through her. What would she do if something happened to them? Everything in her demanded she go to them. It was her fight and she should be out there. Turi stood by the door blocking her passage. Even Tate was near the window, stopping her from trying to peek outside for any sight of what might be happening.

"I can't just sit here." She stood and began pacing the small area. The walls seemed to close in around her as the minutes passed.

"There's nothing you can do. They would just be distracted making sure you were safe, so just sit down. I know my brother, he'll be back soon." Turi tried to reassure her. "How about I tell you about the time Taber, Thorben, and Tad snuck off the island. They took Dad's boat, thinking they'd never be caught and tried to come over to the mainland."

"What happened?"

"Not much. They watched something on the news about a club in Anchorage, and thought Nome must have one they just didn't know about. They weren't too smart back then, and sure as hell not very quiet. Dad heard them, but instead of stopping them he followed with his brother." Turi chuckled before continuing. "They took the boat back, leaving my idiot brothers stranded."

"How did they get home?"

"Leo called Dad," Tad said, opening the door.

Uninterested in the rest of the story, she ran to him, wrapping her arms around him. "You're okay!" Tears streamed down her face. "Where's Milo?"

"Right here, darling." Milo stepped out of Tad's shadow, wrapping his arms around her. "I told you everything would be fine."

"Jeffrey?"

"Dead. He's no longer a threat to you," Tad whispered before pressing his lips to hers.

"Devon was shot in the shoulder. He'll be up once the medics attend to him." Milo took the hands of his mates and led them toward the door. "If you'll excuse us."

She allowed herself to be led away, her heart fluttering. Everything was over, and her life was changing—hopefully in a good way. Weeks ago when all this started, all she could think about was getting her life back, getting back to her job. Now work seemed unimportant. No longer did she care about chasing down the hottest stories in the name of news. All she knew was she wanted her future to include a lot of time with these two men—naked.

The hallway seemed smaller, trying to squeeze down it with two bulky bodies on each side of her. Occasionally an elbow would bump against the wall as they tore off their clothing. Tad's shirt was the first to go because there wasn't a shoulder holster to worry about. Followed closely by hers.

By the time they made it to the bedroom door, she was out of breath and every ounce of her screamed for them. She turned into Milo's body after he sat his gun and holster on the dresser, tugging at the buttons of his shirt. Meanwhile, Tad pressed against her back, his shaft hard against the crest of her butt as he kissed a path along her shoulder and up the nape of her neck.

Milo's hand tangled in her hair, pulling her close to him as he claimed her mouth. The underlying tension that had tightened her men since she met them was gone. Relief that it was over, and she was all theirs without any danger lurking, relaxed them. Exploring his mouth, she realized just how much she enjoyed the connection. It let her feel what they were feeling, keeping her completely in tune.

Her soft moan was muffled only by Milo's mouth as she reached back to touch Tad, her hand gliding along the side of his chest. The hardness of his muscles made her want to turn to him and explore them, to run her fingers along the groves, to feel them constrict as his excitement grew.

Tad unhooked her bra, sliding it down her arms before his fingers found her nipples. Breaking the kiss she threw her head back in pleasure, resting it on Tad's chest. Never before had her nipples held such sensitivity. They felt like a direct like to her core, sending a burning fire of need through her.

"Please, I need you…"

"Who do you need?" Milo asked, a joyful light in his eyes letting her know he was pleased she was enjoying herself.

"Both of you. Take me…however you please." Earlier, she'd thought one would tire of her eventually, that there was no way she could divide her attentions equally between them. In that moment, she knew it didn't matter. They'd find a way to make it work, because it was what they wanted. She wanted them, both of them, in every way.

"Mate, you have too much clothing on." Milo reached down and unsnapped her jeans, tugged them off her, and gently pushed her back onto the bed.

Landing with a flop, she wasn't surprised when the mattress depressed on each side of her. Surrounded by their naked bodies, she reached out to them only to have Tad capture her wrists in one of his large hands.

"Lay back," Tad ordered, slipping his hand between her legs. His finger slipped between her folds, finding the bundle of nerves and teasing them gently. Milo cupped her breasts and gently swirled his thumbs against the hard buds, pinching them. Pain mingled with pleasure and her back arched.

Sparks fired inside her. The sensations collided, sending her head spinning as desire rushed through her. Her legs shook as Tad brought her closer to climax. She sought it with everything she had, wiggling against his hand, searching for the final touch that would send her over the edge.

"Oh no you don't." Tad placed his hands on her hips and rolled her over to slip between her legs. "I want to watch you take Milo while I'm inside of you. I want to feel your orgasm as your muscles tighten around me." He lined up behind her and she shuddered with the contact as he thrust into her from behind, his hips slapping against her ass. Her core ached from their earlier eagerness, making her so sensitive she nearly came again.

Liquid heat melted through her and she stretched out a hand to caress the length of Milo's shaft.

"Come here," she whispered, pulling gently on his manhood.

He slid down in front of her until she was able to take him into her mouth. Drunk on the need to have them both, she swirled her tongue around the tip, sucking it hard, forcing a groan from him. Drawing him into her, he reached down to cup the back of her head, speeding her pace.

As Tad pounded into her, she was able to take Milo's entire length into her mouth, working back and forth until their bodies sang together in perfect harmony. Waves of ecstasy engulfed them, and Milo was the first to cry out as he filled her mouth with cum. She writhed beneath Tad, swallowing Milo's juices as another wild climax spiraled through her. Moments later, Tad cried out as he slammed home a final time and came, filling her.

Tad slipped out, moving to the side of her, his arm still around her. Her body curved around Tad's, Milo cuddling against her back, his arm draped over both of them. Tilting her head up, she met their gazes and smiled. Somewhere in the mix of it all she had falling in love with them, so much that she was willing to give up Texas, the excitement of chasing after the next news story, everything, as long as she could stay with them.

"What has you a million miles away from us?" Milo drew light circles up and down her arm.

"I was just thinking about how much my life is going to change." She paused, trying to figure out how to convey exactly what she was feeling. "Things that meant so much to me before have lost their meaning. It's like I see the world through new eyes. Everything is so bright, there are colors that weren't there before. A quiet evening by the fireplace is now appealing, whereas just last week I couldn't stand an idle moment."

"What exactly are you saying?" Tad pressed.

"That what I thought I wanted all these years, a fast paced journalism career, isn't as important as I thought it was. I don't want to return to Texas. Not if it means losing you two."

"No matter where you want to be, there's no chance of losing us." Milo kissed the nape of her neck.

"I want to stay in Alaska. I don't care if it's right here, the Brown Island, or your compound. Wherever, as long as I have you at my side it will be home."

"Well…" Milo rose up on an elbow and looked down at them both. "I hope you mean that because my Alpha, Ty, has requested my assistance. I was hoping to convince you to come back to the compound once the weather clears. Your mother will meet us there.

I'll give you as much time as I can, but there's an urgent matter in Minnesota I must attend to."

"Urgent matter?" She rolled onto her back so she could see Milo.

"Tabitha has begun to take her place as the Queen of the Tigers. Her first step is to start uniting the tigers as one. In order to do that she needs each clan's Alpha to accept her as a ruler above them. Ty believes I can get the Minnesota clan's Alpha, Calvin, to come around since we have a history together. I gave my word that once the blizzard was over I'd make arrangements to fly there and speak with him in person."

She turned to Tad, sliding her hand down Tad's chest. "Will you go?"

He smirked. "You don't think I'd let you out of my sight now, do you?"

"Tad's our mode of transport anyway." Milo laughed. "All the Brown brothers have a pilot's license, so they tend to be our chauffeurs. There are a few others who can fly among my clan, but with the Browns you get a pilot and warrior in one. You don't have to worry about taking a pilot on a mission who's going to be collateral damage."

"You only claimed me as a mate so you would have a personal pilot at your beck and call." Tad teased Milo.

"You've discovered my secret."

She snuggled against her men, enjoying the easy banter between them. There would be another few days of craziness before things settled down. The visit with her mother would be interesting to say the least.

Oh, how that woman can rub me the wrong way.

There had never been a time they'd gotten along. Her mother might be proud of her as Milo and Tad claimed, but she never said it to Courtney. No, it was always that she could do better if she worked a little harder. The visit promised to be stressful.

* * *

With a string of curses, Milo tossed the phone on the dresser. His damn shoulder injury acting up was a blessing and a curse. It gave him more time with Courtney, but he wasn't there when his clan needed him. He hated being out of the action, even if he was enjoying other exploits.

"What's happening?" Tad stepped out of the bathroom, a towel wrapped around his waist. His hair dripped, sending little rivets down his chest.

"A small group of rogues tried to attack the compound about an hour ago. It's under control now. I believe they've gathered some information from the captured. Taber was shot during the raid. Bethany has healed him, but he's in no condition to fly, not that I think Kallie would allow him out of her sight right now." Milo looked at Tad, thinking of how much the Brown family truly risked for his clan. "Adam will be bringing the helicopter, there's enough of a break in the weather that he'll be leaving soon. Now we don't have to worry about the airport reopening, he can land here."

"My damn family has an attraction to bullets." Tad growled.

"He's okay. Just grumpy, but all you bears are grumpy." Milo did his best to lighten the mood. "I think it's more Kallie keeping him at the compound than anything else. It was too close of a call for her after everything she's been through. Those brothers of yours are like her security blanket. She's been through a lot in her life, you can't blame her."

"No, but I can blame Taber for getting himself shot."

"Who got shot?" Courtney came up behind Tad. Jeans rode low on her hips, a tight tank top stretched tight across her chest and flat stomach. Her long hair was wet and shiny.

"My idiot brother." Tad slipped his arm out, catching her before she could squeeze past him. He tugged her against his body, dipping his head toward her before Milo cleared his throat to stop them.

"Adam will be here soon, so as much as we'd like to go back to bed and enjoy our new relationship I suggest we don't."

"My sweet Milo, always the logical one." She turned to him, smiling.

"I can't help it. Plus, your mother arrived and she's putting up a fit for someone to bring you there or she's coming after you." He glanced to Tad. "Your father and Turi are waiting to speak with you before they return to the island."

"Now why do I have the desire to say 'yes sir' when he say things like that?" Tad smirked before letting go of Courtney and crossing the room to the clothes laid out on the bed.

"Someone needs to keep you in line." Milo adjusted his shoulder holster and slid his gun home. "I need to see to Tate and Hazel.

While I'm gone, please do your best to be ready before Adam arrives. We won't have much time before the second storm hits." He grabbed his jacket and slid his arm into it as he strolled from the room.

He didn't want their time at Lisa's house to end. It would mean he'd have to get back to his duties instead of spending every waking moment wrapped around Courtney's body. Time away made the heart grow fonder, but it also put his beast on edge. The tiger within wanted everything, his duty, his mate, and as much excitement as possible.

Chapter Twelve

The snow had finally begun to lighten, teasing the residents and making them think the storm had passed. It would be back with a vengeance before nightfall. Not long after Tad, Milo, and Courtney had slipped out through the narrow window of time.

"It seems as though I'm losing another son to the tigers." Devon sighed.

"You're not loosing any of us. Taber and Thorben have spent more time on the island than at the compound, so don't give me that, Dad. Milo has some things to attend to at the moment, but as soon as it's over I'll bring them to meet Mom and the others." Tad hated the thought of returning to the island, and showing off his mates when it inevitably meant Aunt Bev would have to attend the family gathering.

"Seems you also put the fear into Turi that he and Trey are next. He's been adamant that he's not sharing a mate with his twin, no matter the costs."

"Dad, you know as well as I do that when he finds his mate it won't matter if he has to share her with Trey or not. Nothing will keep them apart." Tad looked out the window, watching as Tate and

Turi marked a spot for Adam to land the helicopter. "Are you sure you don't want to return to the compound and have Galan or Bethany heal your wound?"

"I'm fine. It's healing on it's own, and it's not serious enough to bother the healers." Devon rubbed a hand over the wound. "If you need us to come with you for whatever Milo needs to accomplish, we can. Trey can manage the sleuth for a short time."

"Thanks. I really do appreciate it, but things are under control. You're the Alpha, you need to be there in case any problems should arise. Plus, Milo has me. What more could he ask for?" Tad joked.

"You're both lucky to have each other, not to mention Courtney. She's a real gem. Ava's going to love her. Another daughter finally coming into the family. She's going to start pestering soon about grandbabies."

"Dad!" He shook his head, unable to believe his father. "We've just mated. Give Courtney time to adjust to shifters and our lifestyle. Maybe you should start bugging Taber and Thorben, they're the oldest. They have the responsibility to give you grandchildren first."

"Then when you bring Courtney to meet your mother I suggest Taber, Thorben, and Kallie come as well. We can make it one big family visit if Theodore can tear himself from the compound too."

His family was unbelievably insane, and their timing was often questionable, but he wouldn't change them for the world. Having a tiger as a mate, Tad had the challenge of getting Milo to accept that the Brown family was part of the deal.

Tiger bonds with their family were limited. Most tiger shifter offspring ended up leaving the clan they grew up in, searching for another one to make their name in. Separating families, across the country. They didn't have the loyalty to a family that their human counterparts did. The loyalty was only to their mate. Parents and siblings were a different category altogether for shifters. Siblings normally remained close despite distance, but parents seemed to drift farther. Most believed it came from their beast; it was how they were in the wild.

When a tiger shifter mated with a human, it was different still because in most cases the family would never know about the ability to shift, or the dangers that shifters had to face. Human families were cut out. Bears shifters were always close, and poor Milo was about to find out the hard way just how close. He was about to be thrown into Brown family drama head first, and soon they would see if he would sink or swim. If he sank, the other Browns would see him as weak, something Tad would never stand for.

"Son…" Devon laid a hand on Tad's shoulder.

"Sorry, what?"

"You were a million miles away, thinking about your mates I presume. Mating is a powerful thing, something that can get an excellent warrior killed if he's preoccupied."

"Nothing like that. I was thinking that we each have something to overcome for this mating to work. At least Jeffery is behind us now." He shoved his hands into the pockets of his jeans and gazed out the window, his thoughts troubling him.

"What has to be overcome for you and Milo?" His father had never been one to beat around the bush. If he wanted to know something, no matter how personal, he asked—especially when it came to his sons.

"Milo has to prove himself by bringing Calvin, the Minnesota Alpha, on board. I highly doubt that it's going to be an easy challenge no matter how much history the two have. Shifters are set in their ways and most are not willing to accept change easily." If he was honest with himself, he was concerned what they were walking into when they made the journey to Minnesota. Their trio was just getting on their feet, feeling their way through this mating blindly. To have a challenge that could be so disastrous right at the beginning made things tense. It would be the first time the three had to work together for a common cause, combining each other's strengths and hiding their weaknesses.

"Milo is a great warrior, and an excellent political member of the clan. Ty wouldn't send him if he wasn't completely confident in him. Having you and Courtney with him won't hurt things either," Devon reassured him. "Now what is it that you'll have to overcome?"

"You, the whole family." He laughed. It sounded so ridiculous now. "Milo's not used to things as we have them. A tiger's devotion is only with his mate. Parents and siblings aren't important, but that matters to me. I can't help but wonder if it will cause tension between us."

"Milo cares more about family than you think." Devon didn't explain, but pulled his hand away. "Look at Kallie, she's a tigress and has accepted our family with open paws. Give Milo a chance and I know he'll surprise you."

Ava and Kallie spoke on the phone nearly everyday. For a tigress that had been kept a prisoner, locked in her animal form, she had made a remarkable transformation since mating with his older brothers.

"I'll keep my fingers crossed, but I doubt Milo's going to have the same bond that Kallie has formed."

"What about me?" Milo's voice came from behind them.

"I'll take that as my cue. Turi and I will be on our way." Devon gave Tad a nod. "Remember what I said."

"Safe travels." Milo held out his hand to Devon.

He nodded and shook Milo's hand. "Welcome to the family, look out for my boy."

Once Devon was gone, Milo wandered over to the window. "I was checking my text messages. So what did I miss?"

"I was telling Dad about the trip to Minnesota." It wasn't exactly lying, though it was a little too close for Tad's comfort when it came to his mates.

"And?"

With a deep breath, Tad decided it was best to get it out in the open. "I'm concerned that you're going to be uncomfortable when it comes to my family. They can be a little overwhelming, especially to someone who's not used to dealing with families."

"It's not like I have no idea what I'm getting into. I've been to the island, family dinners with everyone. I've worked with all of you on missions. I know your family. Nothing's going to be different just because we're mated with Courtney."

"If you believe that, you're in for more of an awakening than I thought." Tad chuckled. "Being family, they will be in your business more than ever. Mom might be the worst, but hell, Dad was just asking when they were going to get grandchildren. Trust me, things are going to be different, they are going to be unbearable. Maybe grandchildren will calm them."

Milo slipped his hand into Tad's. "Things will be fine. Though I have to say I'm not sure how Courtney's going to feel about producing a child as quickly as Ava might like. She still has a lot to adjust to."

"I'm fine with that. I'd prefer to enjoy my mates for a bit longer before there's children brought into the picture. When it happens, it happens. Let's allow things to go naturally for now. If she makes us fathers before we begin trying, then wonderful, if not we can have a lot of fun attempting it down the road." Tad gently caressed Milo's hand. "Anything important in the messages?"

"Yes, Quinn knows that Jeffery has been taken care of. He is less than pleased. He needs to deal with the former accomplice they had an arrangement with, but will be flying to meet with Courtney soon."

Tad nodded. "I figured he'd be angry that a career making case fell apart before he could claim credit for taking Jeffery off the streets."

"Hey everyone, your savior is here! I've come to get you out of this nasty weather. Come sing your praises to me," Adam hollered as he came through the front door.

Milo shook his head, smiling. "Adam, you're so full of yourself since you've found Robin."

"Just wait until you spent a few months with your mates, always at your beg and call, telling you how amazing you are. You'll be just as cocky. Now let's get this show on the road."

"I'll get Courtney, and then we'll be ready. How about you make yourself useful and take the bags to the helicopter," Milo suggested, before strolling down the hallway to where their mate was resting.

"Where is she? I thought she'd be stuck to you two like glue."

"She's laying down, she had a rough night," Tad explained.

"Aww, keeping her busy in the bedroom?" Adam grabbed the bags from the table and turned on his heels.

"There's more to mating than just sex," Tad called after him before he was able to close the door.

"The sex is one of the best parts, though." Courtney smirked at him with Milo just a step behind her. "Maybe we could stay here a few days longer and…" She wiggled her eyebrows at him.

"I'd like to but Ty nearly had to restrain your mother up to keep her at the compound." Tad made his way to her.

"In a few days we'll be in Minnesota and I promise we'll make time to show you just how much we cherish you. With every inch of your body, we'll show just how much you mean to us." Milo brought the hand he was holding to his lips. "But first you must see your mother."

"Speaking of Minnesota, while you were resting we made reservations at a nice hotel in downtown. We thought being off Calvin's land would allow us time without the constant eyes watching us, where we don't have to worry about anything but pleasing you." Part of Tad was looking forward to the trip. He was excited to get his mates alone again.

"That won't make things hard for you, Milo?"

"No, I'll still be able to deal with Calvin. Hopefully it won't take too long, but if I know him as well as I think I do, he's holding out to get something for himself. Now come on, Adam's waiting and your mother's probably driving Ty insane by now."

Tipping his head back, Tad let out a deep laugh. "I'd say so. I've received more text messages than I care to count from her already, and we haven't even taken flight."

"I don't understand her." She slipped her hand into Tad's, holding both of them. "She's acting as if we're close. It's been weeks since we've spoken, and even when we do it's always quick and we don't discuss anything important. Our relationship is basically nonexistent."

"Your mother loves you, and has missed you. She talks about you all the time. I don't know what drew you two apart, but maybe this is the opportunity you need to rekindle the relationship," Tad suggested, before pulling her toward the door.

Chapter Thirteen

Courtney's hands sweated and her stomach turned as Adam sat the helicopter down on the compound's landing strip. Her mother stood not more than twenty feet away with two men. It was almost enough to beg Adam to fly them away. She wasn't ready to deal with her mother, and maybe she never would be.

Leaving home had been the one thing that made her grow up. No longer was her mother there being overbearing, driving her crazy at every move. She had come into herself, and she wasn't willing to go back to the way it was.

"It's going to be fine," Milo reassured her. "Lisa is only worried about you."

She wanted to say that her mother never worried about her, only tried to control her. That was all she did her whole life, why would this time be any different? Instead she kept her mouth shut and nodded for Milo to open the door. She took Tad's hand in hers and gave it a squeeze.

"We're right by your side, always." Tad gave her a quick kiss before releasing her and letting her slip out of the helicopter.

"Courtney!" Lisa called through the slow whipping of the blades as the helicopter shut down. She looked the same as when Courtney took off to Texas, the same attitude of control radiating off her. Her short curly hair framed her face, making her look younger than she actually was.

Courtney looked to Milo and took his hand for comfort.

"Mom, it's good to see you." Her mom rushed forward, wrapping her arm around Courtney. Instantly, every muscled in her body tensed.

"Oh baby, I'm so glad you're okay." She stepped back and looked behind Courtney. "Taddybear." She held her arms open, waiting for him to come to her.

"Lisa, it's a pleasure to see you again."

"Thank you both for keeping her safe." Lisa stepped back, looking at the three of them.

"We can't take all the credit, but what matters is she's here." Tad placed his hand on the small of her back.

The gesture helped calm her, but had the opposite affect on her mother. Lisa's eyes widened, and she took a step backward.

"I explained this, Lisa." A man with shoulder length black hair stepped up next to her. The hard look in his eyes and the way he carried himself made it clear he was in charge.

"That's Raja, the clan's Lieutenant. The other man is Marcus, his brother-in-law," Tad explained.

"It can't be." Lisa's voice trembled. "I don't want this for her."

"Lisa, I told you Tad, Milo, and Courtney were mated. I tried to warn you before they arrived. What you want doesn't matter in this case, it was Courtney's decision and it's clear what she chose." Raja tried to calm Lisa.

"No, I won't have it. I had such big plans for her."

Courtney let out a deep exhale. "Mom, stop this. This is my life. I make the decisions for myself now."

"You don't understand what you're getting involved with. Did they even tell you what they are? The danger that they possess, that surrounds them? Damn it, Courtney, this life isn't for you."

"I know all about it, and I've made my decision. Now if you'll excuse us, we would like to see Tad's brother and assess how he's healing." She nodded to Tad, who led them around the still wide-eyed Lisa and toward the buildings.

Raja's voice rang out behind them. "Lisa, if you continue to act as you have, I'll have you returned to your house in Nome. You might be a close friend of the Browns, which is why we've opened our home to you, but I will not stand for you to discriminate against my members. Courtney is now a member of this clan through her connection with Milo and Tad."

"She's my daughter!" Anger heated Lisa's voice.

Milo glanced back, frowning. "Lisa is not putting herself in the good graces of the clan with her comments," he said sadly.

Courtney tensed. "I'm sorry if her attitude causes problems with your Alpha and Lieutenant. She does this wherever she goes."

Milo gave her hand a gentle squeeze. "No, if she continues to stir trouble the Elders will force her to leave. We have too much happening at the moment to concern ourselves with someone who is against us because of what we are."

"I've known Lisa for years and never realized she had an underlying hatred to our kind. After I've looked in on Taber, I'll speak with her to see what has her so angry." Tad looked off into the distance for a moment before continuing. "I thought Hazel might have told her years ago that we were to be mated. I thought that's why she came up with that little nickname for me."

"Don't worry about her, she has insane mood swings. I wouldn't be surprised if in an hour she finds us and welcomes you to the family with open arms. She's always been like that." She glanced to each of them. "It doesn't matter to me. I've made my decision, I want to be with you both, nothing will change that. In a few days she'll be gone and I won't hear from her for months. We've never been close, no matter what she tells people."

"She's still your mother. Someday that relationship might be repaired. We'll do what we can to make sure there isn't a grudge because of us." Milo stopped and pulled her close to him. "Love means making sure your mate is happy. If we have to deal with a little anger from Lisa while she accepts this, we will."

Tad moved to stand in front of them, not touching but watching them closely. "We love you, Courtney."

"Oh Tad!" She reached out to him and drew him into their embrace, tears formed in her eyes. "I already realized I'd fallen in love with you two. I just couldn't bring myself to say it for fear I'd lose you."

"You won't ever lose us." Milo wrapped his other arm around Tad and they stood there as minutes passed by, none of them wanting the moment to end.

After years of being alone, she had finally found where she belonged. She belonged with them, preferably naked in bed snuggled between them. Finally, everything was falling into place.

Tad kissed her forehead. "Come on, let's get you out of the cold."

"One last thing. With my mother acting as she is, that's not going to cause problems with your clan accepting me, will it?" The fear of not living up to what the clan wanted from her made her voice shaky. If they didn't accept her, it could cause problems for Milo and tension between them.

"There's no reason to concern yourself with that. The Elders and the clan won't hold any of Lisa's action against you." Milo caressed her cheek with the backs of his fingers. "Everyone is going to welcome you with open arms. You have nothing to worry about, sweetie."

"Are you guys going to stand outside all day or actually come in and introduce us to your woman?" Looking toward the voice, there was a man standing on the porch. It had to be one of Tad's brother. The dark hair and build was nearly identical.

"Thorben." Tad took hold of her hand and led them forward. "How's Taber?"

"A cantankerous fool." Thorben opened the door as they neared.

"Quit making a bad impression on our new family members." Another male voice called from inside the house, sounding as irritable as Thorben had described.

"It's okay, darling, I swear he doesn't bite." Tad pulled her along with him as he made his way inside to where Taber was laying on the sofa, his mate with him.

"Don't lie to her." Thorben plopped down on the chair closest to his mates, rubbing his forearm. "That bastard has a ferocious bite."

"Hey, I don't want to know what goes on behind closed doors." Tad looked appalled by the thought.

"Shut up, Tad. I bit Thorben when he pulled out the bullet. The bastard did it while I was unconscious. He got what was coming to him." Taber shot a look at Thorben, one that was full of daggers.

"Ignore them. I'm Kallie, I'm sure you've already gathered this rather irritable man is Taber, my other mate." The woman between the men shook her head, drawing Courtney's attention. The white streaks in her long curly brown hair made her wonder why anyone would want such striking highlights.

She forced her gaze away from the woman's hair and focused on Kallie. "I'm Courtney, but I guess you already knew that."

"Don't be nervous, we're family. Have a seat and make yourself at home."

Tad led her around to the other side of the sectional, Milo coming up behind them. "How are you doing, Taber?"

"I'm fine." Taber growled. "I wish everyone would stop hovering."

"We only hover because we love you." Kallie smoothed her hand over his shoulder. "He was shot in the chest, just missing his heart. Too damn close for my tastes, but it was a through and through shot. A lot of blood was lost, so he's supposed to be resting for a few days, to give his body time to heal the remaining injuries Bethany wasn't able to heal."

"You said Thorben pulled the bullet out," Milo said, confused.

"He was hit in the shoulder as well, that's what Thorben pulled out," Kallie explained over Taber's growling, as she laced her free hand through Thorben's.

"You're supposed to miss the bullets, you dumb animal." Tad scolded his brother.

Before Taber could come up with a witty comment, Kallie spoke up. "Bears are big targets, he was easier to hit than us sleek tigers." She winked at Milo.

Courtney nodded in understanding. "You're a…"

"Tigress," Kallie supplied. "I change into a white tigress, hence the white stripes in my hair."

"Milo doesn't have orange highlights from his tiger. Does it only affect women?"

Deafening silence settled over them, making her feel uncomfortable before Thorben scooted closer to Kallie, wrapping his other hand over their already joined ones. "Kallie spent years locked in her tigress form. Thankfully for us, she didn't lose herself to her beast. The consequences for those years show in her hair."

Courtney swallowed, feeling awful she asked. "I'm sorry."

"It's fine." Kallie smiled. "I don't like to talk about my life before I met my mates, but as you can see it's part of me. Hell, it's what led me to find them, and I wouldn't change that."

"Dad tells me you almost thumped Turi. What did the boy do now?" Taber ran his hand down his mate's arm, clearing willing to change the subject to ease her discomfort.

"That idiot brother of ours cornered Courtney and started to tell her about Rosemarie. I ended up telling them." Tad laced his fingers through Milo's, bringing the trio's connection to its fullest. "It wasn't his place. I swear that boy's never going to learn to keep his mouth shut. If anyone gives away the family secret, it's going to be him."

"Turi's always been the most open and outspoken of us. He should have come to you before going to your mate, but it needed to come out. They deserved to know." Taber yawned.

"You need rest for your body to finish healing." Tad rose, bringing Milo and Courtney with him. "The day after tomorrow, we're going to Minnesota to attend to some business for Ty, but when that's done we'll be back. Just don't get your stupid ass shot again."

"Give it to him," Taber ordered, looking back at his twin.

"We've arranged for you to have cabin twelve." Thorben stood, pulling a key from his pocket. "Milo's place is too small for the three of you, and this cabin is at the far end of the compound close to the creek and near us." He tossed the key to Tad.

He left go of Courtney's hand and caught the key midair. "Thank you."

"There's enough room for your cabin to be built next to ours if you're going to make this your home. It would be nice to have you guys as neighbors. I'm sure Courtney and I will be close friends in no time, as we try to escape from the four of you," Kallie suggested. "If you're going back to the island, I'm sure Mom would be thrilled to have you."

With a smile, Tad glanced to Milo. "Actually, we've agreed to stay here. Milo's position in the clan means a lot to him, and Dad isn't giving up his role so there's little we can do for the sleuth now anyway. When we return from Minnesota, we'll speak to the construction crew."

"Very good. Have a safe trip if we don't see you before you leave," Kallie called after them as they left.

Outside, Tad looked down at Courtney. "I want you and Milo to go to the cabin, I need to find Lisa and see what got her so worked up."

"Don't worry about her."

"I must, this is so unlike her." He dropped the key into her hand. "I'll be there soon."

"If he can help Lisa see what she's doing, it's worth a try. Come on, sweetie." Milo slid his arm around her waist and led the way to the cabin as Tad made his way in the opposite direction.

"This is stupid, she'll never see what she's doing."

"He has to try, as I would if I was in his shoes. You're our mate, and no matter how much you deny it her actions affect your happiness. You just want her to let you live your life, to care about your happiness. If Tad can get that to happen, it will make you feel better. He's doing it for you." Milo's fingers teased along the waistband of her jeans. "That's our cabin."

She looked to where he nodded. A charming log cabin sat nestled amongst the trees. A large porch dominated the front, and a few feet away a creek flowed, the sound of the water instantly relaxing her. "It's beautiful."

Quickly climbing the steps to the deck, she was anxious to see what the inside looked like. Milo slid the key into the lock, pushed the door open, and stepped back. She was overwhelmed by the space. It was larger inside than she thought it would be. She stepped inside, moving out of the way so Milo could get out of the chilly air. A large cream sectional stretched in front of a fireplace, acting as a divider to the kitchen. It was very open and airy. The creamy brown walls added character and color to the place, and drew out the warm tones of the hardwood.

She wandered toward the kitchen, where the warm honey color wood cabinets highlighted the gold of the granite countertop. A gourmet six burner stove and double ovens made her smile. It was everything she needed to make delicious sweets for her men.

"There are two bedrooms in the back. Does it suit you okay for now?"

"It's perfect." She turned to face him. "Two bedrooms?"

"Yes. This cabin is normally used for visitors. Why?"

"I just thought..."

"Just because they're there, doesn't mean they both have to be used." He smirked and came toward her, quickly picking her up and setting her on the counter. "My amazing mate." He kissed her, claiming her as his again.

Two for Protection: Alaskan Tigers

Chapter Fourteen

Tad watched as Lisa paced the room. He had been there for over ten minutes and still hadn't gotten any useful answers out of her. She was furious that Courtney had mated without consulting her mother first.

"Lisa, please sit down and tell me what the hell has you so worked up."

"Worked up? You bastard…you let my only daughter mate with *him*." She spit out him as if it was a bad word.

"Milo?"

"Don't you stand there and act like you don't know what I'm talking about. How could you?"

He ran his hand over his face, completely put off by her attitude. Taking a deep breath, he reminded himself he was doing it for Courtney. "Lisa, it wasn't your decision. Mating is stronger than anything you've ever felt before, but even with that she made her decision. I don't understand what you have against Milo, and frankly I don't care. He is our mate. What I do care about is what you're doing to Courtney."

"What *I'm* doing? What about what he will do to her?"

"She is in no danger, she has two mates to protect her."

"Bullshit." She threw the glass in her hand at the wall, shattering it.

If he didn't get her under control quickly, Ty would have her removed from the grounds. "What do you think he's going to do to her?"

"I've heard what tigers do to their mates. She won't survive the first time he's mated with her. You're going to let him kill my daughter!"

He almost laughed at the absurd idea. "Not that it's any of your business, we've already mated with her. Nothing's going to change the fact that Milo and I are your daughter's mates. Now I don't know what you've heard, but obviously they're lies. You've seen her for yourself, she's uninjured."

She stopped pacing and stared at him. "Tigers are dangerous."

"And bears aren't?"

"Damn it, Tad, how could you let this happen? Hazel told me she'd end up with a bear and another. I assumed it would be a human or another bear. Not a tiger. Courtney deserves a normal life, not surrounded by danger. At least with you, she'd be safe on the island. She's my only daughter, I don't want her killed because your kind has enemies."

"I think your problem is that you can't see us as anything but animals." Tad narrowed his eyes. "You're referring to us as if we're inferior. We're people just like you and we deserve to be treated as such."

"Your family might be close to human, but the rest of these animals…they're just that, animals."

Before he could suppress it, a growl vibrated the walls. Anger and hurt welled up within him.

"See!" She pointed to him, her eyes wide. "You're an animal. Humans can't do that. I'll tell the world what you are if it means getting my daughter back. They'll destroy this compound as soon as the news hits."

"You have been a friend of my family for years, but now your true nature comes out. I believe you would do just as you threaten, even if it meant your daughter's life." He pulled out his cell phone, pressed a couple buttons, and brought it to his ear. "Ty, I need a guard for Lisa, and if you could meet me at cabin twelve, there's something that needs to be discussed in the presence of my mates."

"I'll send Styx and meet you there."

"I'll wait for Styx, then I need to swing past and grab Thorben so I'll be there in ten minutes." He ended the call and met Lisa's gaze. "You have created this mess, and you'll have to deal with it."

* * *

With a roaring fire warming the cabin, Courtney snuggled against Milo. The only thing missing was Tad. She slid her hand under his shirt, exploring his chest, wanting him naked. Suddenly his body tensed under her touch.

"What is it?"

"Ty…" His words where cut off by a knock at the door. "Come in."

A man with dark shoulder length hair stepped in and Milo stood, clearly surprised to see his Alpha. "What do we owe this to?"

"Tad asked me to meet him here." Ty came around the sofa. "Welcome, Courtney."

"Thank you." Hesitantly, she took the hand that was offered. "I hope my mother isn't causing too many problems for you."

"I believe that's what Tad has asked me here for. He was collecting Thorben, but should be here soon."

As if summoned by the statement, the door opened and in stepped Tad, with Thorben on his heels. "Ahh, Ty, thank you for coming." Tad shook Ty's hand before coming to her, taking up her other side. "Let's sit."

"Is everything okay?" She was trying to figure out what her mother had done and how it was going to affect her, all the while trying to remind herself that in less than forty-eight hours they'd be on their way to Minnesota, far away from Lisa.

"I'm afraid there's been an issue with your mother, and I've gathered us all here to make a decision." Tad spent the next few minutes filling them in on what had happened. His voice held so much sympathy as he watched how Courtney was handling it.

Her stomach roiled, and her heart broke. Her mother would honestly rather see her dead than with the men she loved. "She'll have to be asked to leave." Courtney's eyes brimmed with tears and she wrung her hands in her lap.

"I'm afraid it's beyond that now." Ty dragged his hand through his hair. "She's a security threat."

"What does that mean?" She met Ty's gaze, hoping he didn't mean they'd kill her. She might not be that close to her, but she didn't want her to die either.

"She'll tell the world our secret, it's the reason we don't normally tell humans. Lisa found out by accident, but it has to be fixed. It's why I wanted you here for this discussion. Being that she's your mother, I wanted you to have a say." Tad took her hand in his.

"You don't mean she has to die..." Courtney took a deep breath, biting her lip.

Ty shook his head. "Not if there are other options."

"Maybe if Tabitha speaks with her? Explain what we're trying to do. Where is she anyway?" Milo leaned forward, placing his hand on her leg.

"No, that wouldn't work," Ty said. "We can't risk her knowing any other secrets. Tabitha and Bethany are cooking, or she'd be here. They're making food to take to Kallie. Since she doesn't cook and Taber is laid up, they offered." Ty glanced at Thorben, raising an eyebrow. "Two bears eat a lot."

"Hey, I could have cooked," Thorben snapped.

"Umm, could we get back to my mother?" Courtney wanted to scream, but instead she clenched her fists in her lap. "You said other options, so what are they?"

"Three options." Tad squeezed her hand. "Hazel could remove Lisa's memory, or she could be kept here in complete isolation."

"The third." Her throat tightened, knowing what the last one was. She needed to hear it.

"Her death."

"I don't understand why I'm here," Thorben said.

"Our family is deeply involved in this," Tad explained. "If Lisa tells our secret, then the island is in grave danger. I'm emotionally and physically invested in Courtney, and depending on her decision we might need someone to think logically."

She made a small sigh. "Then remove her memory of shifters. It's the best option. Living in isolation isn't a life and it's worse than death." She let out the breath she was holding.

"It's not that easy." Milo pushed off the sofa and stalked to the window. Waves of guilt poured off him and into his mates. "Removing her memory of shifters, our mating, and anything that has to do with Tad's family means you can't see her again. Seeing you again would trigger those memories, forcing us back to the position we're in now. Hazel will have to replace the memories of you with something else."

"Those aren't options. No matter what is chosen, she loses."

Ty nodded. "It's the reason Tad said you had to be the one that makes the decision. She's your mother. Are you willing to give her up so she can live the rest of her life?"

"What if I talked to her, maybe I can…oh hell, she's never listened to me. This won't be any different." The tears she had been holding back fell. "What about Hazel and Tate? Won't their presence as her neighbors trigger the memories?"

"Yes, which is why they will have to move. Tate's mistake, and their choice to tell her what he is, is now affecting everyone. It's trickling down to everyone who had contact with her since then. Lisa will lose a big portion of her life, and because of that she can't be relocated so she doesn't come into contact with them. Instead Hazel, Tate, you, the Browns, all of you have to stay away from her." Ty leaned back against the sofa. "We'll have to put someone else in Hazel's home to watch over Lisa to make sure she isn't remembering anything, if this is what you choose."

"What about Kenneth?" Milo suggested.

"He'd be a good choice. He's a former Special Forces solider, and would be able to keep tabs on her without seeming suspicious. Plus, he owes us." Tad turned to her. "First, you must make your final decision."

"You make it sound like I have a choice. No matter what I choose, I'm about to lose my mother. How can I make this decision?"

Milo stared outside. "I'm sorry, this is my fault."

"How?" She brushed away from Tad and went to him. "Milo." She placed her hand on his back and still he didn't look away from the window.

"This was brought on because of the rumors she heard of the tigers. She might have never shown this side of herself if you had only been mated to Tad."

"That's doubtful," Ty interjected. "Tad has been working with us, and within time Lisa would have found out. She would have eventually made her hatred known. I'm just thankful it was before she was able to tell anyone our secret."

"See, this isn't your fault."

Milo turned to her and wrapped his arms around her, pulling her close. "You shouldn't have to deal with this."

"No one should have to deal with this." She took comfort from Milo before glancing back to Ty. "Wipe her memories, with the condition that I'm allowed to see her before you do."

"I'll take you," Tad offered.

"With that settled, I'll make arrangements for Lisa to be transported back to Nome where Hazel can clear her memory. It's best to have it done in her home since she'll sleep for hours once the ritual takes place. I'll have Kenneth and his family take over Hazel's house." Ty stood. There was a deep sadness in his eyes when he glanced at her. "Courtney, you have my sympathies. I know this isn't an easy decision, but Lisa will be able to continue her life without a threat to any of us."

"It must be done to keep the secret. I can't risk losing Milo and Tad." She pressed her face into Milo's shirt, unable to hold back the sobs that shook her body.

"Oh, sweetie, I'm sorry, don't cry." Milo smoothed his hand over her back.

The front door shut, and seconds later she felt another hand caress the small of her back.

"Darling, I'm sorry," Tad whispered.

Chapter Fifteen

With her heart breaking, Courtney stood at the airstrip trying to make the goodbye with her mother end on a good note. Lisa believed she was only going to Minnesota and then would come back to her, but Courtney knew the truth. This would be the last time she would ever see her mother, feel her arms around her. The woman who had given birth to her, and had driven her insane more often than not, would be out of her life for good. There was a freedom mixed in with the unending loss.

"You okay to do this?" Tad asked, placing a hand on her arm as Lisa approached with Styx directly behind her, acting as her guard.

"I have to." She nodded and stepped toward Lisa. *Keep it positive, let her know you love her, that's it. Don't fight with her.* Instead, she wanted to scream about the injustice being done. Having to choose between the men she loved and the only family she had was impossible. "Mom…"

"Don't take that tone with me, child. It's out of the question for you to go with them. I won't stand for it, now I want you to gather your things and come back with me."

With a deep breath, she bit her tongue, refusing to scream at her mother. Instead she decided to stick with what she'd rehearsed. "Decisions and commitments have been made, and I'm going to Minnesota. I'll think about what you said about Milo while I'm gone. When this is over, I'll come to Nome and we can discuss it further. Please...I don't want to fight with you."

"What about while you're there? He could kill you before you even have a chance to return."

"Mom, Tad will be there. He's not going to let anything happen to me." Not denying that Milo might hurt her went against everything in her, but it was Milo's idea in an effort to avoid an argument.

"Lisa, you asked me to protect Courtney before, this is no different. You realized I would lay my life down in order to protect her. Trust that I will keep her safe now and always." Tad stood next to her, making it hard not to reach out and touch him.

The not touching part had been another of their ideas. If Lisa saw them embracing, it would only be a reminder that Courtney was also mated to Milo. She hadn't realized how hard it was not to share in those little gestures.

"Everything is going to be fine, Mom. Tad needs me to go to Minnesota, but I'll be back soon. In the meantime, I need you to go back home. I'll come to you when I can."

"You'll come home?" Surprise was clear in Lisa's voice.

Home? Yes, she'd come home, just not the home Lisa expected. She'd come back to the compound. It was her home now. There was nothing left for her in Texas, and even less in Nome. By the end of the day, Lisa wouldn't even know Courtney. The plan was to leave her with a memory of her daughter passing months after the graduation ceremony. Kenneth, his sister, and his niece had already taken over Hazel's house and would be there as her friends. Everything was in place, but none of it made parting any easier. Not bothering to clear up the confusion, she nodded.

"I have to go. I love you."

"I love you too, and I just want what's right for you." Lisa stepped forward, wrapping her arms around Courtney.

Blinking away the tears that filled her eyes, she returned the embrace. The last embrace.

She had no idea how long they stood there before Tad cleared his throat, but it didn't seem long enough. All the frustration she held for her mother, the anger over being controlled, never being able to do the right thing, none of it seemed to matter anymore. For the first time since she was a little child, there was peace between them.

"I have to go."

Lisa nodded. "Stay safe."

She turned to the plane before the tears began to fall. Making her way across the tarmac, she knew when she broke down and grieved, her men would be there for her.

"Keep her safe, Tad." Lisa called out to them as Courtney hurried up the plane steps.

"She's in good hands." There was a hint in his words that Lisa missed, letting Courtney know he wasn't just talking about himself but also about Milo. He pulled the steps up, giving them privacy, and in that moment she couldn't hold the tears back any longer.

"Oh, sweetie." Milo rushed down the aisle to her, wrapping his arms around her.

"I'm okay." She spoke through her tears and buried her face against his hard chest. Tad came up behind her, folding his warm body around her back.

* * *

The plane glided through the air smoothly, making good time even with the delay. In no time they'd be in Minnesota giving Milo a chance to appease Calvin's demands. After making sure the blanket was snuggly around Courtney's sleeping form, he made his way to the cockpit. Tad would want an update on their mate; he'd been reluctant to leave her when she was in distress, but someone had to fly them to Minnesota. Arriving late wouldn't make their job any easier, especially not with Calvin who would use any excuse to get out of Tabitha having a say in his clan.

"How is she?"

"She wore herself out and is finally sleeping peacefully."

"You know this isn't your fault." Knowing just what Milo was feeling, Tad tried to reassure him. "If Tate hadn't told her of the secret, she'd have never known. He didn't just give away his secret, but my family's, which wasn't his to tell."

"Tate has some blame in this, but we have to deal with the consequences. Courtney lost the only biological member of her family. Even us, the sleuth, and the clan won't replace that."

"Nothing can replace the bond between a mother and child, but this was the best option we had. Would you have risked your whole clan, my family, all of the shifters to keep Courtney and Lisa in contact when they already had a very strained relationship that might not have survived Courtney's search for her own freedom?" Tad glanced over his instruments before looking over at him again.

"When you put it that way…" He glanced out the window, not that there was anything to see but blue sky and large, fluffy clouds. "It doesn't change the guilt."

Milo turned to find Courtney standing in the doorway, her face still stained with tears and the blanket wrapped around her shoulders.

"There's nothing to be guilty about," she said, her voice soft. "My mother made her own decisions. No words can take away what I know you're feeling, but I don't blame you. Like my mother, I also made my own decisions. I chose you, both of you."

Milo leaned against the co-pilot's chair and held out his hand to her. When she took it, he pulled her tight against his body and whispered, "I love you."

"I love you too."

"What about me?" Tad teased.

Still locked in Milo's embrace, she reached back and touched Tad's shoulder, his head tilted enough to lay a kiss on the back of her hand. "I love you too, my very own Taddybear."

"Tonight I plan to show you how much I love you, but we're approaching our decent. Milo, you have just enough time to make your phone call if you're quick. So sit down and buckle up."

"Can I stay up here? I always wanted to see a landing from the cockpit." She pushed away from Milo enough to look out the window.

"Sure. Take the co-pilot's seat. That means you're alone in the back, Milo."

"No problem. I need to call Calvin and let him know. We'll stop at the hotel first, check in, and change before meeting with him." He leaned in and kissed a very excited Courtney before she could slip into the co-pilot's seat. "Have fun."

"Oh, I will. I always wanted to do this. Could you teach me to fly? I think it would be so amazing." There was an exhilaration in her that he'd never seen, and it made him smile.

"When we get back, I'll teach you anything you want." Tad winked at them both before Milo left.

Making his way to one of the seats, Milo let go of the tension he had been holding when it came to Courtney, only for it to be replaced by the stress of dealing with Calvin. The Minnesota Alpha could be an ass, and at that moment Milo didn't have the patience to deal with games. He wanted the Minnesota clan committed to Tabitha so he could return to his mates.

Taking his seat, he pulled out his cell phone and called Calvin.

"Hello?" A deep voice answered.

"Calvin, it's Milo. We're coming in for our landing now. We'll check into our hotel, freshen up, and should be there…" He glanced at his watch, quickly doing the math for the time change. "By seven."

"No." Calvin growled. "You'll be here by twenty minutes after six or don't bother coming. We will be having drinks at six-thirty."

"That will be cutting it close." He should have known Calvin would try to worm his way out of meeting with them that night.

"Be here or we'll try to meet tomorrow. Your choice, but make the right one or your Queen might be upset you failed." Calvin hung up.

He squeezed the phone, wanting to shatter it in his hand. Calvin would test all of Milo's patience and then some. It would take everything in him not to ruin this. With the Elders depending on him, he had to find a way to make it work. Hopefully, Courtney and Tad would be the strength he needed to get through it.

Two for Protection: Alaskan Tigers

Chapter Sixteen

They had been at the hotel only ten minutes, but their time was up. If they were going to make it to the meeting, they had to leave right away. Courtney fluffed her hair and strolled out of the bathroom.

"Let's get this show on the road, because I was expecting some time with you two before we had to rush off to meet this Calvin."

"As was I," Milo admitted, chagrined. "When we made the reservation, the meeting with Calvin wasn't until the next day. Since then he kept changing it, and this last time he demanded we be there now or not bother coming. If you want to stay here…"

"I'm not letting you deal with this alone. I might have no experience with shifter business, but Tad said we're stronger if we're together. So let's go, but you'll be making it up to me later." She grabbed her leather coat off the chair where she'd tossed it.

"Will I?" Milo raised an eyebrow at her before glancing at Tad. "Seems our mate is becoming demanding."

"I knew she'd fit into our world just fine. She's not going to take shit from anyone." Tad shrugged on his jacket before opening the door.

"Damn right. Now let's get going." She held her hand out to Milo. "You're going to be fine. Who can resist us when we work together? We'll let you take the lead, and with each of us playing off each other's strengths we're bound to succeed."

"I hope you're right."

"I'm a woman, I'm never wrong." She smirked at him.

He took her hand and walked to Tad. "Just remember, he'll use whatever he can against us so let's not give him any ammunition. I opted to stay at a hotel off his land and that offended him, but since we are here representing Tabitha he can't force the issue."

"You're worrying too much." She reminded him, because it was starting to put her on edge.

"I'm used to guarding the Elders, not acting on their behalf. This is new territory for me. It should be Tad doing it, at least he has more experience with this since he represents Devon."

"You're the one with history with Calvin," Tad said. "Use that to our benefit, and I'll be there to help you with the rest. Now we've got to go or we'll be late." He closed the door behind them, and forced them onward.

She took a few calming breaths and tried to share her ease with Milo. He was wound tighter than a prodded tiger in a cage. Even Tad's and her touch seemed to do little to calm him. With luck, the first meeting with Calvin wouldn't go badly and things would be easily resolved.

* * *

Milo let Tad drive so he could sit in the back with Courtney. Her touch helped relax him, and he needed to prep himself. Whatever happened with Calvin could be disastrous to the Alaskan Tigers. If he didn't submit to Tabitha's command, then it made him an enemy—a dangerous one. The Minnesota clan was double the size of the Alaskan Tigers, making them a large threat.

Nevertheless, Milo's clan would have the upper hand. With the Kodiak Bears, Texas Tigers, and West Virginia Tigers completely devoted to Tabitha, there was little doubt they wouldn't be able to handle whatever issues arose. Tabitha also had her magical book that had been guiding her along the path to becoming Queen of the Tigers since meeting Ty. It would warn them if anyone planned to attack, giving them a chance to be ready.

Tad parked the SUV and glanced in the rear view mirror at them. "Ready?"

"No." Milo laughed. "Let's do this anyway."

"There are already a few gathering. Courtney, come out Milo's door. I want us all on the same side if anything happens."

"If they threaten us we're within our right to demand their lives." Milo glanced out the tinted windows at the gathering, searching the crowd for Calvin who was nowhere in sight. "Even Calvin isn't stupid. He knows if any of us are hurt on his land, Tabitha will demand he steps down as Alpha."

"That only matters if he's truly considering joining Tabitha."

"What are you saying, Tad?" Courtney asked.

"Have either of you considered we might be walking into a trap? Calvin might have agreed to this meeting as a swipe at Tabitha. It's possible he thinks this is a way to make Tabitha appear weak."

"Thanks, Tad." Milo shook his head. "That was just what I needed."

"I want you to be prepared. Courtney, here's the spare key to the SUV." Tad reached back, handing them to her. "If anything happens, don't worry about us. Get the hell out of here. In the glove compartment there's a satellite phone, press and hold two and it will call someone to come and get you to safety."

Milo raised an eyebrow. "Who?"

"I didn't walk into this without being prepared. Theodore is waiting nearby in case shit goes wrong. He can get Courtney to safety."

"Theodore, as in your youngest brother?" She slipped the key into the pocket of her black dress pants.

Tad nodded. "I know you'll be safe with him."

"Thank you, I should have thought of it." Milo shook his head.

"You were wrapped up in everything that was going on." She squeezed his hand.

"There's no excuse, I risked your life and that's unacceptable."

"She's right, you were concerned with other things. I had it covered and it doesn't matter who thought of it, only that she'll be safe if things go off track." Tad turned back in his seat. "More are coming."

"We should go." Milo took a deep breath and opened the door. Quickly he stepped out before reaching back in and taking her hand to help her out. He kept his gun hand free and positioned her to his left, just slightly behind him. Enough that she was protected without making it appear he was being too cautious.

"You're cutting it close for my Alpha's preference." A platinum blonde stepped out of the crowd wearing a sleek, black pinstriped business suit. "I'm Tina, his personal assistant. Now if you'll follow me, I'll take you to him."

Aghast that Calvin had his own personal assistant, Milo wondered if he was that far removed from his own clan that he needed one. Taking the lead, Milo made sure Courtney was slightly behind him with Tad, keeping the crowd's interest focused on him rather than his mates. "I explained to Calvin that we would do our best to be here, however the weather in Alaska gave us a delayed start."

"You should have arrived last night to be in time for him." She spoke as if he was royalty, her total dedication clear.

"That had been the plan until Calvin made changes and requested we appear tonight."

Tina stopped and spun around to face them. "You *will* address him as Alpha."

"We will do no such thing, he's not our Alpha." Milo glared at her, wanting to put the woman in her place. He was not a member of this clan, but he still outranked her. Tad and Courtney, feeling his anger, placed their hands on his back, and he swallowed the unsaid words. "Take us to Calvin or we will leave and you can explain to him why we're not there. If you wish to bring his temper down on you, so be it." Milo waited a brief second, and when she said nothing, he turned to his mates. "I will not play games with a low member of this clan. Let's go."

"No, no, don't go." Tina stumbled on her words. "I'll take you to him. Follow me." She quickly climbed the steps.

"You're doing great." Courtney reassured him before they started after Tina.

They followed her through the building, taking no notice to the people who gathered in the hallways to catch a glimpse of them. What had Calvin told them?

At the end of a long hallway, Tina stopped and turned to them. "Wait here while I announce you." She quickly opened the door, stepped in, and shut the door behind her.

Milo took Courtney's hand in his, caressing it. They had been led too far into the house for Courtney to get back to the SUV if things became dangerous. There didn't seem to be any other exits once they'd made it to the third floor. She'd have to get down the steps at the end of hall and through all the shifters gathered around the first floor, along with the ones outside. She stood no chance alone. It only left him with one option; he couldn't let things get out of control.

The door creaked open. "Come in, the Alpha will see you now."

Milo wanted to slap the assistant, and scream at Calvin. It was clear he was brainwashing his members, since they always referred to him as Alpha and never by name.

Inside the room, it was clear how expensive Calvin's tastes were. The space was open, with lots of windows looking over the grounds. No doubt he'd watched them arrive.

"I expected you five minutes ago." Calvin lounged on the leather sofa.

"We'd have been here if your assistant hadn't detained us." Milo stepped forward, taking Courtney and Tad with him. "Calvin, I'd like you to meet my mates…"

"I know who they are and I don't care. You should have left them at the hotel."

"I told you they'd come with me. If you didn't like it, someone else could have been sent here to discuss your concerns." There was no way Milo would have left them behind as targets while he was detained with Calvin. "Shall we get down to business?"

"Tina, bring us four whiskeys," Calvin ordered, not answering Milo's question.

"None for us."

"You must join me in a drink."

Milo shook his head. A drink wasn't something he wanted; he only wanted this to be over, and it was impossible to know what Calvin would mix into those drinks.

"We've had a long trip, and a drink will only make us tired. Can we just attend to business?"

"It is rude to refuse the drink of an Alpha." Calvin glared at them.

"At one time I might have been naive to the rules of clan life, especially when it came to the Elders and their guards, but no longer. You cannot pull the wool over my eyes." He met Calvin's stare with one of his. "It is only rude to refuse refreshments of one's own Alpha, and you're not my Alpha. But if you wish to go that route, I will point out that it was rude to request that we come tonight, instead of waiting until tomorrow once we've had time to rest."

"I see you've grown into yourself." Calvin took the whiskey Tina offered, swallowing it in one sip before handing the glass back to her. "Fine, if you want to get on to business, tell me why Tabitha is determined to make herself the ruler over all tigers."

Milo nodded, and the three of them sat on another sofa across from Calvin. "Tabitha is destined to bring us together for our sake. One day we'll be able to live in harmony among the humans. Wouldn't you like to live without having to worry if someone finds out our secret? This world would allow us to be as one to fight those against us instead of standing alone."

"Having humans know about us means nothing to me. They are lesser creatures than us. If we're going to announce we live among them, we should put ourselves in a position of power over them."

"I won't stand for you speaking that way about them. Courtney is a human, and there are many others I know who are dedicated to our kind." Milo took Courtney's hand. "Now if you will explain to me what is holding you back from committing to Tabitha, then we can get started."

"I wasn't able to stay this over the phone, but I will commit this clan to Tabitha as the Queen...*if* she's willing to assist me with some minor details." Instead of reaching for another whiskey from Tina, he grabbed the bottle.

"Committing to the Queen of the Tigers isn't for personal gain."

Milo couldn't believe what he was hearing. Surely his only friend hadn't completely lost his mind, thinking he could manipulate them to give him what he wanted.

Two for Protection: Alaskan Tigers

Chapter Seventeen

Milo took a deep breath and slid to the edge of the sofa.

"If you're trying to use us to get something you want, it's not going to happen. We will take our leave now, and will leave your land tomorrow. I have not come here to compromise a deal where we will be manipulated."

"You do not understand." Calvin took another long swing from the whiskey bottle. "I need your help to keep my clan. There is much uproar within my ranks and I'm losing control. There has already been on attack on my rule, and my Lieutenant was killed in the attack. I have another forty-two hours before I must announce a new Lieutenant."

"Why? What's the reason your members are trying to overthrow you?"

Calvin finished the bottle and handed it to his assistant. "Another one."

"Calvin?" Milo had begun to wonder if the clan wasn't trying to overthrow him because of his drinking problem. Shifters had to drink a lot in order to get drunk and even then it would wear off quickly, forcing him to drink more to stay drunk. Or it might be his attitude, as Calvin always believed he was superior to everyone else.

"I do not know, only that they want me out of power." Calvin sat the bottle down with a heavy bang. "There are still some among my clan that are loyal but not enough to keep my position. My life might not be as important as yours is, but I do not wish to die."

"We're not here to make you a stronger Alpha, you have to keep your position yourself." Milo wanted to shake Calvin for his stupidity. Instead of proving himself as an Alpha, he had barricaded himself on the third floor. While they waited for a chance to kill him, Milo was sure someone else had already begun to take on the role of Alpha within the clan. There had to be a new group of Elders forming floors below, while his former friend sat up here drinking and feeling sorry for himself.

"Then what good is this commitment to the Queen if she won't help the Alphas following her?"

"We'll help you with your enemies, but when it comes to you keeping your command that is something that you must do. You won't be respected if someone else has to step in and take control of your clan." Milo looked around the room before continuing. "Hiding out here isn't going to make your problems go away. If anything it will make them worse."

"What would you know? When have you ever had people depending on you?" Calvin screamed at him.

"He's not the same young tiger you once knew." Tad finally spoke. "The changes in Milo from when he first joined the clan until now make him a completely different person. His role in the clan is one of authority, he has people depending on him."

"I smell the bear within you." Calvin rose and stalked to the window. "Your word means little to me, you know nothing of living in the clan."

"Seems you should have done your research." Tad smirked. "On the contrary, my family is very different than other bear sleuths. We are very much like the Alaskan Tigers, and more to the point I've been spending more time at the compound than on my sleuth's land. I've accompanied Milo on missions that saved countless lives, and have protected our kind from the dangers that haunt us."

"You're not a tiger, you'll never understand." Calvin didn't look back at them, only continued to stand his ground. Milo's old friend needed a wakeup call.

"Tiger, bear, wolf, or lion, it doesn't matter…we all have the same problems." Milo had grown tired of Calvin's outdated views, and he was growing irritated. "Maybe the tigers are dealing with a different aspect right now with the rogues continuing on with Pierce's plans, but we all have a common enemy of hunters. If humans find out about us without some preparations, we will be hunted down and killed or worse yet used for experiments. None of us want that, which is why Tabitha's claimed her destiny. Either you are with us or you're against us. It's your choice."

"Help me then." Calvin begged, the nearly empty whiskey bottle sagging in his hand, ready to slip through his fingers. "I have a large clan that could be at your disposal if you assist me in keeping my position. Do this and I'll make my commitment to the Queen of the Tigers."

"That is not something we're doing. I explained what joining us would mean for you. Being against us, your clan will be seen as an opponent. Choose to go against us and I vow you'll lose your position." He nodded to Tad and Courtney, his gaze drifting to the door to make it clear they'd be leaving.

He let Tad lead the way with Courtney close by, and he took up the rear before glancing back to Calvin. "Old friend, it's time to grow a pair and defend your title or step down before they kill you."

They were nearly at the staircase when a deep growl quaked the building, shaking the pictures on the wall, vibrating the glass in the windows. "Go!" Milo ordered, ready to draw his gun if any of the clan members took this as a signal to attack.

Running down the three flights of steps, they hurried back the way they came. Everyone who had gathered to watch them enter was gone. Milo tensed, the eerie emptiness making him uncomfortable. Where were they?

With the front door less than fifty feet away, Milo almost let out a sigh as they rounded the last corner—until he saw where everyone had gone. Three large men were blocking the door, while at least twenty other men positioned themselves around the large foyer. Women and children were missing from the gathering, making things more dangerous.

Milo and Tad circled Courtney, placing her safely between them, and neither of them pulled their weapons even though they were ready to. Milo faced the men in front of the door who were clearly in charge.

"We have no problems with you, we only want to leave. There's no need for anyone to get hurt here today."

"We're not gathered to hurt you, only to warn you." The shortest of the three laughed.

"Silence, Aaron." The man in the middle, who wore a freshly pressed suit, stepped forward. "I'm Christian, and I know who you are." He held out a hand to Milo.

He took the hand that was offered. "What is the meaning of this?"

"Calvin has been keeping things very close to the vest, hiding out on the third floor and neglecting his duties. Your visit was only announced this morning or you'd have been contacted already."

"What are you getting at, Christian?"

"The clan is tired of walking on egg shells around Calvin. His moods fluctuate too drastically, and it's time for a change. We have a battle on our hands that you don't need to be a part of."

Milo nodded. "We have no desire to get involved with it, that is your clan's business. We're only here representing Tabitha, Queen of the Tigers."

"I'm well aware she has taken hold of her destiny." Christian looked to the men who stood by the door before he turned back to face Milo. "I believe you had planned to be in town for a few days to get things arranged with the clan. If that's still correct then once this business tonight is taken care of I'd like to meet with you to discuss the standing of the Minnesota Tigers."

"We'll be here for a few days, and I'll gladly sit down with the new Alpha whenever it's convenient." Milo took Courtney's hand, leaving his gun hand free in case things changed. "If you'll excuse us, we've had a long journey."

Christian waved his hand and the men standing in front of the door stepped aside, holding it open. "I'll send word when things are complete and I'm ready to meet with you." He moved out of the way, leaving them to pass without issue.

Without delay, Milo led Courtney outside, Tad watching their backs as they quickly made their way to the SUV. It had been bad timing to come in the middle of a fight for control.

Milo slid in beside Courtney in the back, leaving Tad to get behind the wheel. They needed to get off the clan's land and back to the hotel before Christian and his followers decided it was an opportune time to deal with Calvin.

"Shouldn't we warn Calvin?" Courtney asked.

"No. It's their business. If he had control of his clan, he wouldn't allow this to happen. He knows their intention so if he's strong enough to keep his position he'll be ready. Otherwise, another Alpha will be in control of the clan by morning." Milo watched out the window as the SUV sped away.

"You're not bothered about his death?"

"It is our way." He smoothed his hand over her leg. "When you take a position in power, you know the risks. If an Elder does not have the authority to keep his members under control, he has two options—step down, or fight to the death. If he steps down, he'll keep his life as long as he doesn't interfere with the new ruler."

"It's so barbaric." She tucked a strand of her hair behind her ear. "Wouldn't it be easier if there were a vote to elect a new leader?"

"I love how liberated you are, my love." Tad smiled back at her in the rear view mirror. "We're too old fashioned for that."

Milo wrapped his arm around her, snuggling her against his body. Loss was a part of life, maybe more so since they were shifters. Even with death all around him, it made him sad that within hours his friend would lose his life because he was too stubborn to see the truth. Milo never thought Calvin would have made a good Alpha, and was surprised a clan the size of Minnesota followed him. Still, seeing him crumble was disappointing.

"Are you okay?"

"My ever caring mate." He ran his hand down her arm. "I was just thinking about the Calvin I knew years ago. He's not the same man anymore. He's so broken there's almost nothing left."

* * *

Night had fallen over Minnesota, bringing the bright skyline, and Courtney stood there taking it all in. Milo had been reserved since returning to the hotel. The tension poured along the connection into each of them, forcing them to deal with his dark mood.

Tad came up behind her, his arms wrapping around her waist until his body was tight against her back. "Give him time, he'll work through it."

She nodded, placing her hands over his, lacing their fingers together. "I know, it's just hard to see him suffer and there's nothing I can do."

"Losing a friend from childhood is difficult, especially when they have the chance to save themselves and do nothing."

"Isn't there anything we can do?"

"I'm afraid not, love." He hugged her tighter.

They stood there, each of them locked in their own sadness, while on the other side of town Calvin might be dying. It was a rude awakening to this new world. Would she lose her men like this one day?

"Tad…" The words caught in her throat.

"What, love?"

"Could it come to this one day for us? Will I lose you as Tina will lose Calvin tonight?"

"Tina and Calvin are not mated."

She thought back to Tina's expression when she looked at Calvin, the devotion, the pain over what he was doing to himself. There was something between them. "But I saw such adoration in her eyes."

"That might be so, and she might love him on some level, but they are not mated."

"You didn't answer my first question."

He spun her around to look at him. "I can't tell you it will never come to that. Shifters live long lives, as do their mates even if they are human. The mating bond ties you to our life span. That being said, many things change through the years. Milo and I are not in the position Calvin is in. Milo is one of the Elder guards, so he's in danger on missions, protecting the Elders, and many other clan activities, but there wouldn't be any challenges to the death."

"What about you?"

"Taber and Thorben are the first born, so they're destined to take over my sleuth when our father steps down. If they choose not to, it would fall on me. For now, that isn't an issue. Now I'm helping Ty and Tabitha with whatever they need. Yes, that means I'm in the same danger as Milo, but like him there'd never be a challenge to my life because I don't rule over anyone." He ran his hand through her hair and cupped the back of her head. "There's nothing to worry about, we're going to be with you for a long time."

Every ounce of her wanted to believe him. She could feel the truth in his words, but that little voice in her head screamed she could lose them. It was amazing how in such a short time not only had she fallen completely in love with them, but she couldn't picture her life without them.

Two for Protection: Alaskan Tigers

Chapter Eighteen

Milo sat in the chair he'd pulled close to the window as he debated whether or not to call his Elders while his mates slept peacefully in the bed. He'd been putting it off, but Ty needed a report. The lights decorating the sky bounced off Courtney's naked body as she snuggled tightly against Tad. Milo had done his best to join them, but the thoughts racing in his mind wouldn't quit.

The Elders had depended on him to get the Minnesota Tigers on board as an ally. Instead, he wondered if their presence had made things worse for Calvin. Everything in him wanted to go back to the complex and knock some sense into Calvin. That idiot would rather die than give up his position.

His cell phone vibrated in his hand, a text message lighting the screen. *Report. Received word of gunfire in Minnesota.* Unable to wait, he slipped from the bedroom and called Ty.

"Is everyone okay?" Ty demanded.

"We're at the hotel."

"Then you're unaware there's something going on at the complex."

Loyalty to Ty had him explaining things as if they didn't matter to him. "Unaware wouldn't be the right word. Calvin is in no position to govern the clan. Either our presence provoked this, or it was a coincidence, regardless it seems there will be a new Alpha in charge of Minnesota by morning."

"Then you should return until things have calmed."

"As we were leaving our meeting with Calvin, there was an incident."

"Incident?"

"We were cornered by a group of the male clan members, and Christian seemed to be in charge. He warned us this didn't involve us. Which is when I explained we wanted nothing to do with it, we were only there representing Tabitha. He made it clear there'd be a new ruler by morning and asked me to stay to meet with him."

Ty made a displeased noise that had Milo rethinking things for a moment. "I don't like you there when things are still unsettled within the clan, especially with Courtney. If you walk into a trap, she's an easy target."

"We're very aware of that, but I don't believe we're in any harm. If I believed she was in danger, we'd already be on our way back home." Milo leaned against the sofa in the small living room off the bedroom. "I believe the clan is already following Christian. The men with him were looking to him for guidance. I'm under the impression Calvin's been having some issues with his clan for a while. It's gotten difficult enough that he barricaded himself on the third floor."

"Interesting. It doesn't make sense that he wanted someone to come to him to discuss joining us if he knew there was such an uproar with his followers."

"Actually, he had hopes to blackmail us into forcing his members to follow him. Either that or he wouldn't commit to Tabitha. He believed we needed his clan enough that we'd do this for him."

Ty's deep laughter seeped through the line, lightening Milo's heart for a moment. "I hope you told him…"

"That we'd do no such thing. If you'll allow us to stay here I believe I might be able to get Christian as an ally."

"Very well. If you need additional backup, give me a call. I know Theodore is already there, and there's others I can call who are closer to your location and are loyal to us if you need them."

"Thank you. I'll be in touch when I have more information, and hopefully good news." Milo felt the weight being lifted off his shoulders with his Alpha's anger no longer a possibility. "If I may ask, how did you become aware of gunfire at the complex?"

"I told you there are those loyal to us. Minnesota has a number of members who are devoted to Tabitha, and if their Alpha doesn't commit they're willing to leave the clan to come here or to another devoted clan." The happiness was clear in Ty's voice. "My mate has many supporters for her cause. Unfortunately, some of them are in hiding because of their own Elders, but with time hopefully that can be changed."

"I had no doubt Tabitha would take the tigers by storm. We couldn't have chosen a better person to do what she's going to do if we were able to pick."

Ty laughed again. "Hurry back. Kallie and the women are planning a welcome dinner for Courtney. They want to make her feel at home with all she's been through."

"Have things been taken care of with Lisa?"

"Yes. Hazel wiped her memories. Kenneth and his family are now Lisa's neighbors, which worked out nicely since we needed a place to put Kenneth so we could keep an eye on him. With him knowing our secret, he might be valuable to us. Also, Hazel and Tate are currently staying at the Browns' island, until they can determine what to do."

The bedroom door opened, letting light in from the window, revealing Courtney. "Are you coming back to bed?"

Ty must have heard her. "Go back to your mates. She'll have a life she couldn't have without you, so never doubt that fate did the right thing by making her your destiny. Don't feel guilty. Jeffery would have killed her if you and Tad hadn't been there. Remember that next time the remorse returns." With that, Ty hung up.

The Alpha was always in tune with the members of the clan. The stronger the connection and devotion, the stronger the Alpha's bond, which explained why Ty knew what Milo was going through.

He locked the phone screen and looked at Courtney. Her body was wrapped only in a sheet, making him instantly hard. He held out a hand to her, and without hesitation she came to him and pressed her body against his.

"Is everything all right?"

"Ty only wanted an update." He reassured her, enjoying the feel of her body against his.

"That isn't what I meant." She pulled back enough to look at him. "We've all been through a lot these last few days."

He nodded. "You more than any of us."

"See, I was going to say *you* more than any of us." She pressed a finger against his lips before he could remind her of Jeffery, Lisa, and all the shit they'd overcome. "I don't need to be reminded. Let's just say you're feeling it the most. The guilt over what had to be done before we came here, now the loss of Calvin. Everyone makes choices in life, and when those decisions are made people have to live with it. Calvin made his, and we have to make ours. Letting Calvin tear you apart like this isn't healthy. Instead, let me show you how much you mean to me." She let the sheet drop away from her body.

His shaft hardened, straining against the thin material of the shorts he'd thrown on when he got out of bed. She dropped to her knees before him, sliding her hand down the front of the shorts to take hold of his manhood. Gently tugging it out, her hand caressed the length of him.

"Love." He tried to pull her back up to him.

"Let me." She leaned forward, kissing the tip of him before letting him slip between her lips. Taking him between her lips, her hand worked at the base, and he tangled his hand in the strands of her hair, holding her close.

Her mouth worked up and down the length of him, milking the life out of him. Each move made him weak.

"No." He nearly screamed, when all he wanted to do was let her finish. Her gaze drifted up to him. "Not like this, I want to be inside you."

She let him slip from her mouth, and he pulled her up, lifting her to the back of the sofa, his fingers pulling her legs apart until he had the access he needed. His tiger refused to wait, and with one powerful thrust he slid into her welcoming opening. She was tight without the foreplay, making each thrust full of contact both pleasurable and painful.

His teeth grazed along her neck as he worked himself deeper into her, her cries of frustration filling the room, mixing with his own moans. With each thrust, his heart sped with need and desire.

"Milo." She clenched her legs tightly around him.

He pressed his lips over hers, claiming her cries with his mouth. Their breath became ragged as he rocked in and out, finding the perfect rhythm, bringing ecstasy within reach. His balls tightened with need, and he held his breath, waiting for her to find her release before he allowed himself his own.

"Oh, Milo." She screamed, throwing her head back as she tightened around him and her body exploded with pleasure. He continued to drive his shaft into her, until with one final slam home his own release followed.

He held her against his body, his shaft still nestled deep within her as they calmed.

* * *

Her breath had just begun to return, when a throat cleared behind them.

"I sleep, and the two of you are having fun without me." Tad stood in the doorway, his arms crossed over his chest, his own member standing at attention, a smile teasing the corners of his lips.

"Come to me." She whispered and Milo moved to the side.

"I'm not sure I can live up to the performance I just witnessed." He came to stand in front of her, his hands finding her hips.

"There's no judging."

He quickly lifted her off the sofa and lowered her onto his shaft, before spinning around to press her back against the wall. "Still, I'll do my best to make sure my mate is pleased." He lowered his head into the nook of her shoulder, trailing a line of kisses along it until he reached her mouth. Claiming her lips, he held her and drove himself into her.

He intensified the pace, driving the tempo fast with each pump. The thrusts became deeper and faster, moving with precision.

Tension stretched her tighter until she came.

"Tad!" Tipping her head back, she cried out, digging her nails into his back, arching her body into his. He pumped twice more and shouted her name. Exhausted, she sagged against the wall and Tad's body.

"I think we wore her out." Tad glanced back at Milo, clearly satisfied with himself.

"Yes. Bed. Cuddle," she demanded between gasps for breath.

Chapter Nineteen

Loud banging woke Courtney from a deep sleep. She grumbled in annoyance. They hadn't slept very much, and their bodies weren't used to the time change. Opening her eyes, she glanced at the red glowing numbers of the bedside clock; it was just after seven o'clock in the morning.

"Stay in bed, I'll deal with it." Milo kissed her cheek before slipping out from under the sheet.

"It's Quinn." Tad mumbled.

"I can deal with the black panther, and his anger." Milo pulled on a pair of jeans. "There's no use in all of us getting out of bed."

"I don't believe Quinn will see it that way."

"Well, I for one don't care. You're staying in bed with me." Courtney ran her hand along Tad's chest, and Milo's jealousy poured over them. "Hey, you're the one who offered to get the door." She snuggled into Tad.

"The sacrifices I make for the two of you." Milo left with a huff.

"We're going to owe him for this." Tad ran his hand along her spine in lazy strokes.

"*He* offered."

"True, but Quinn is pissed at us and Milo's willing to take the brunt of the anger so we can stay cuddled in bed."

Knowing Milo's intention made her make a mental note to reward him later. "It's unfair he should have to deal with it alone." She slipped out of bed, grabbing a robe as she went. "I'm going out there."

"I thought we were going to stay and keep the bed warm." He stood and slipped into his jeans.

"I can't believe you! You went against everything I told you." A deep voice cut through the air as Courtney and Tad stepped into the living room.

"Courtney, meet a very irritated U.S. Marshal, Quinn Evans," Tad said.

"Irritated?" Quinn snapped. "No, I'm beyond that. I'm livid! How dare you two?"

"I would suggest you keep your voice down if you don't want the neighbors to hear you." Milo sat on the sofa, watching Quinn, allowing him to have a fit before attempting to defend himself.

"I told you I needed him alive and you don't listen. Now his accomplice is on the verge of walking free."

"We did what we had to do, you've read the reports." Tad followed her around the sofa to Milo.

"I should bring you both up on charges."

Courtney narrowed her eyes and glared at him. "How do you plan to do that when Sheriff Lutz and, at the time, deputized Devon Brown have already stated it was done in order to save the sheriff's life? Would you have preferred another person be killed just to keep your case alive?"

"Finding them gave you spirit, Ms. Mathews."

"Jeffery had too many dead bodies in his trail, and no one was able to stop him before. Why do you think that trial would have been any different? With an eye witness, and DNA evidence, he was *still* out on bond harassing me." She took Milo and Tad's hands in hers. "From where I'm standing, they did what needed to be done to save not only the sheriff and Devon's lives, but also mine, and anyone else that crossed Jeffery. They should be rewarded, not hounded because of your case."

"You do not understand the families need justice," Quinn argued.

"They got their justice with his death. He can't hurt anyone else. You're just pissed this case slipped through your fingers because it could've made your career."

"Where was this courage of yours when he was hunting you down like a deer?" Quinn scowled at her.

The hatred in his eyes told her she'd made another enemy. Maybe not one who would try to kill her as Jeffery had, but an enemy all the same. If their paths crossed Quinn's again, it wouldn't be a happy reunion. He would never forget this.

"That's enough, Quinn." Milo stood. "If you're going to attack our mate, then you can leave."

"I'll leave because I've had enough of your righteous attitude. Shifters are not above the law, and they can't kill people whenever they see fit, and orchestrate things so it looks like it was done in self-defense. There *will* come a time when I can see shifters behind bars for their crimes." Quinn spun around and stormed out the door.

"Dramatic much?"

Milo glanced at her before chuckling. "Quinn can be described as many things, but that is definitely at the top of the list. He doesn't like his plans messed with, even if they work out better than he could have hoped. Sheriff Lutz mentioned that Texas had pressure to drop the charges, from people in high places. Jeffery was extremely well connected. It's how he got off the hook from his other brushes with the law."

Knocking on the door stole her opportunity to comment. "It can't be Quinn again." At least she hoped not.

"No, not Quinn." Milo stood.

A split second later, Tad pulled her to her feet and placed her behind him. "What's going on?"

"Just to be safe," Tad reassured her as Milo opened the door.

"Christian, I expected a call not a personal visit."

"I wanted to inform you of the changes myself. May I come in?" Milo nodded, stepping back and allowing Christian and another gentleman to enter. "This is Greg, my Lieutenant."

"It would seem congratulations are in order." Milo shut the door and stepped away. Courtney realized he was staying away from them to make it impossible for Christian to kill both him and Tad at once if things worsened, while staying out of Tad's way if he needed to pull his gun.

"I gave Calvin the chance to step down, but he refused. Unfortunately, Tina…"

"Is she okay?" Milo asked. "I can get a healer here quickly."

Christian shook his head. "During the fight, Tina tried to defend Calvin and she was killed. It was an unfortunate and saddening incident. She was a valued member of the clan until she began spending all her time with Calvin."

"I'm sorry for your loss." She stepped to the side of Tad, enough to see Christian.

"Thank you." He nodded and turned to Milo. "I understand why you're protective of her, but we come here in peace. I would like to speak with you about our commitment to the Queen of the Tigers."

"Very well please be seated." Milo waved his hand to welcome them to the two chairs.

Courtney ran her hand along Tad's arm. "If you'll excuse me, as I'm not really needed for this, I'd like to get dressed."

"I apologize for coming this early, I had hoped to catch you since later I'll be busy dealing with things."

Christian didn't need to explain; not only did he have to establish rule, but he also had to bury their fallen members. Or rather, former members, since Calvin had lost his fight for dominance.

* * *

The sun was beginning to sink again, but this time it felt like the first day of forever. Everything had fallen into place, and the following day they'd be back in Alaskan. Milo had brought Christian and the Minnesota Tigers on board, giving Tabitha and their clan a strong ally in the Midwest. It also gave Milo more confidence in himself and in what he was doing.

In the end, each of them had overcome their own troubled pasts. They were her mates. Their strengths and weaknesses worked well together, each of them playing off the other to form a prefect trio.

"What's on your mind, love?" Tad nuzzled her neck.

"Just thinking how far we've each come in such a short time. I love you both."

"As we love you." Milo's fingers teased along her jawline.

She had no doubt about that. They had already proven how much they cherished her.

Instead, she whispered, "Then show me…"

Marissa Dobson

Born and raised in the Pittsburgh, Pennsylvania area, Marissa Dobson now resides about an hour from Washington, D.C. She's a lady who likes to keep busy, and is always busy doing something. With two different college degrees, she believes you're never done learning.

Being the first daughter to an avid reader, this gave her the advantage of learning to read at a young age. Since learning to read she has always had her nose in a book. It wasn't until she was a teenager that she started writing down the stories she came up with.

Marissa is blessed with a wonderful supportive husband, Thomas. He's her other half and allows her to stay home and pursue her writing. He puts up with all her quirks and listens to her brainstorm in the middle of the night.

Her writing buddies Max (a cocker spaniel) and Dawne (a beagle mix) are always around to listen to her bounce ideas off them. They might not be able to answer, but they are helpful in their own ways.

She love to hear from readers so send her an email at marissa@marissadobson.com or visit her online at http://www.marissadobson.com.

Two for Protection: Alaskan Tigers

Other Books by Marissa Dobson

Tiger Time

The Tiger's Heart

Tigress for Two

Night with a Tiger

Trusting a Tiger

Jinx's Mate

Two for Protection

Storm Queen

A Touch of Death

Snowy Fate

Sarah's Fate

Mason's Fate

As Fate Would Have It

Learning to Live

Learning What Love Is

Her Cowboy's Heart

Half Moon Harbor Resort Volume One

Winterbloom

Unexpected Forever

Praise:

Alaskan Tigers

Tiger Time:

This is the first book that I have read from Marissa Dobson and it definitely won't be my last. I loved the tiger shapeshifter aspect of this book which I haven't read much about in previous books. ~ Jennifer at Books-n-Kisses

When I first read a review for Tiger Time, I knew this was a must read. Now I know that it is definitely a must read for anyone that like were romances. It's definitely one of those that draws you immediately into the story, and never lets you go... a wonderfully written story of a woman's journey into the unknown and a man who would show her to her destiny. LOVED IT!!!! Looking forward to the next one in the series. ~ Addicted to Romance

The Tiger's Heart:

This book was so interesting and I loved it. Steamy with lots of twists and turns. Recommend this to anyone who likes Shifter type books. ~ Amazon Reader

Tigress for Two:

And the plot thickens. I am really enjoying how the overall story arc of this series is going. There are so many players that it is fascinating to watch the plot unfold. Everyone's story is connected, but not in the ways that I had originally anticipated and that makes it all the more fun to read. ~ Delphina Reads too Much

Wow, Tigress for Two was everything I'd hoped it would be after reading some of Marissa Dobson's other books. She packed a whollop, enticing the reader with angst, suspense, romance and suspense…oh did I say that twice? Well good cause I meant to, because she did a great job of keeping the reader in suspense throughout the whole story. I never knew what was coming next but I was so intrigued I couldn't put the book down. I seriously never imagined mixing shifter species but it was done well. ~ A Passion for Romance

Jinx's Mate:

This story was interesting and exciting. I always enjoy story lines with the more exotic shapeshifters since they are so rare in the world. ~ Rande Amazon Reader

This was a good fast paced book…didn't stop until the end. ~ Bobbi, Amazon Reader

Trusting A Tiger:

This series just gets better and better with each addition. The characters get more intriguing and the plot thickens. I just can't wait for the next installment. Well done Ms. Dobson.~ E.A Allen (Amazon Reader)

I can only say I really enjoyed this book. I could not put it down. ~ Eva, Amazon Reader

I sped through this book just like the rest of the series. I can't seem to get enough of Ms. Dobson and her books. ~ Martha, Amazon Reader

The story sequence is uncanny, the author kept the stories but with an individual twist.~ Amazon Reader.

Stormkin Series

Storm Queen:

To use the word amazing is not too strong when describing this book. I've never read anything like it and I loved every minute of it. Do yourself a favor of buying this book, if you don't you'll be missing out. ~Rebecca Royce, bestselling author of the The Westervelt Wolves.

This was a great new addition to the paranormal romance world, it almost had a Urban Fantasy feel because the sex wasn't the main focus of the story and I LOVED that! I thought each scene was done so well! I will be continuing this series! I can't wait for the next one! ~ Amazon Reader

Clearwater Series

Winterblom:

I found Winterbloom to be a sweet and delightful little romance. Ms. Dobson does a wonderful job of creating visual scenes that allow the reader to feel as though they are right there within the story. ~

Unexpected Forever:

Unexpected Forever made me cry. I'll admit it; I teared up quite a few times actually…Marissa has yet again written an amazing story full of emotions and detail. I totally recommend reading Unexpected Forever and other great works by Marissa. ~ Crystal Out There

Fate Series

As Fate Would Have It:

This book has all 3 of the Fate Stories in it! Each are about mountain lion shifters and finding their mates! All are sweet, Heartwarming, Romantic stories! I can't wait to read more by Marissa Dobson! ~Amazon Reader

Snowy Fate:

This was a very quick read, but with just a few pages, Marissa Dobson is able to get to the heart of this story. ~ Cocktails & Books

I really enjoyed Snowy Fate. I hope that you take the time to learn that no matter how hard you try you can't fight fate. ~ Books-n-Kisses

I thought this one was just perfect in length. There was enough background that I felt I knew the characters well and their attraction was believable. Fate has a way of making a HEA very real. I definitely recommend this one! ~ From the TBR Pile

CPSIA information can be obtained at www.ICGtesting.com
Printed in the USA
LVOW11s1957160614

390268LV00001B/351/P